SMOKE AND MIRRORS BOOK 3

MYSTERY AT THE BLACK CAT CLUB

JAN JONES

SMOKE AND MIRRORS BOOK 3

MYSTERY AT THE BLACK CAT CLUB

JAN JONES

Where the floor show is the least of the surprises

~*The third in the Smoke and Mirrors mystery series*~

DEDICATION

This one is for Kate Johnson

A lovely friend and a very good writer

DRAMATIS PERSONAE

Opening Characters

Jack Sinclair ~ a surprisingly busy playboy

Lucy Brown ~ a temporary typist

Rick Brown ~ Lucy's middle brother, vet

Douglas Brown ~ eldest brother, stud manager

Aidan Brown ~ youngest brother, medical student

Harry Brown ~ Lucy's father, racehorse trainer

Basil Milcombe ~ racehorse owner

At Paul Kent Architects

Christina Kent ~ architect and practice manager

Paul Kent ~ her brother, also an architect

Garth Kent ~ their father, retired architect

Vilho Koivisto ~ senior draughtsman

Miss Reed ~ senior typist

Miss Hodge ~ junior typist

Mrs Corrigan ~ married typist

Elsewhere in London

George Forrest ~ a banker with interesting associates

Youssif Arama ~ manager of the Black Cat club

Rose Garden ~ leader of Kitten Kaboodle dance troupe

Daisy Brickett ~ timid dancer

Enid Bursall ~ prosaic dancer

Mr Trelawny ~ elusive commodities broker

Mrs Antrobus ~ part-time clerk at Consolidated Cocoa

Julia & Amanda Lester ~ wealthy socialite twins

Theo Nicholson ~ amiable viscount, engaged to Julie

Hubert Jarmaine ~ amiable viscount, engaged to Amanda

Jimmy Ward ~ financial wizard

Gina Ward ~ his wife, former film actress

Tufty Thomas ~ foolish nonentity

The Police

Detective Chief Inspector Curtis ~ of Scotland Yard

Detective Inspector Maynard ~ of Scotland Yard

Detective Sergeant Fenn ~ photography expert

Detective Sergeant Draper ~ fingerprint expert

CHAPTER ONE

Newmarket, October 1927

As the 10.20 race day special from St Pancras to Newmarket shook off the last of the new suburbs, Jack Sinclair let down the carriage window a couple of inches.

"Nothing like a breath of country air to put us in the right mood for a day out."

The young woman in the green suit sitting opposite wrinkled her nose. "All I smell is smoke," she said. "Careful you don't get covered in smuts. I'd so much rather you were presentable the first time I introduce you to my family."

Jack shut the window again. "Would they mind? You said your mother was delighted you were engaged."

Lucy gave him an old-fashioned look. "She's delighted I'm engaged. She'd have preferred it to be to someone with a respectable job and a discernable supply of income. Ideally someone who didn't disappear for a month shortly after I made the announcement."

"I did apologise for that."

"It's not that I worry about my brand new fiancé being sent somewhere secret that I'm not allowed to ask about," said Lucy with patent insincerity, "but if I'd known, I'd have held off telling everyone."

"I am sorry. It wasn't my choice, but it was a chance to follow up a lead involving something I worked on a while ago for Uncle Bob."

She gave a splutter of laughter. "Jack, you are ridiculously easy to tease. I said it was a family emergency and hoped they didn't see any of the picture papers running that photo of you in top hat and tails at a roulette table in Cannes."

Jack winced. "I thought I'd turned my back on that photographer. How did you know it was me?"

He received the impish smile that did terrible things to his self-control. "You have just told me. You must be slipping. It's not often I can catch you out like that."

"Minx. I should know better than to tangle with a writer of detective stories."

She folded her gloved hands demurely in her lap. "As Lucy Brown, I am a humble typist at Paul Kent Architects."

"You are now," said Jack. "Six weeks ago, you were a chambermaid. And before that you were a nippie in a Lyon's tearoom and a playroom attendant on an ocean liner. If I was your mother, I'd worry about you."

"I daresay she would if she knew. On the other hand, the jobs paid the rent, even if that wasn't the purpose as far as I was concerned."

"Game and set to you. Never let anyone tell you common-sense isn't sexy. Earning whilst doing book research is sheer genius. Your family do know about your writing?"

"They don't know about Phoebe Sugar, the celebrated society gossip columnist, but they know about the books. They really would worry how I was paying the rent otherwise. Mother thinks the Lois Barrabell career-girl stories are lovely. Her favourite is *Janey Jones: Nursery Nurse*. She's not nearly so keen on the Leonora Benson detective novels, so she was quite amenable to the suggestion that she doesn't tell any of her friends I write them. I'd never get any research done if people knew about me."

Jack shook his head. "And I thought my life was complicated."

Lucy raised her eyebrows. "You? Posing as a carefree playboy whilst working undercover for your uncle at Scotland Yard? Also clandestinely writing hard-hitting journalistic features as Jonathan Curtis? Piece of cake."

He grinned. "I was right. We are made for each other."

"We might even prove it if we get to spend any time together," said Lucy.

"I wanted to this week," said Jack, injured. "You were working."

"You were the one who suggested I get a job in an architect's office as research for the book after next. I didn't intend to - or not this soon, anyway - but you were called away, and there was a job advert in the newspaper for a temporary typist starting immediately and..."

Further down the corridor an exuberant buzz of conversation drew closer. Jack and Lucy exchanged a wry look. "I fear we are about to have company," said Jack. "May I join you on your seat so our fellow passengers won't hear you coaching me on how to behave with your parents?"

"As if you need it," replied Lucy, tucking her handbag between her and the window. "My father will be too busy with his horses and owners to catechise you, and Mother will be occupied looking after grandchildren. That's why I chose today."

"Fiendish," said Jack.

"Experienced," replied Lucy.

At Newmarket, Lucy gave their fellow passengers time to vacate the carriage before she and Jack collected their belongings and stepped down to the platform.

"This way," she said, walking in the opposite direction from most of the race-goers. They were streaming down to the High Street, to the many hotels and public houses eager to fill customers with liquid refreshment before the races started.

A dozen yards up the road was a familiar pony trap with an even more familiar driver.

"Rick," she called, pleased but suspicious. "Why aren't you up at the course doing your veterinary duty?"

"I will be shortly. One of Douglas's mares is showing signs of discomfort. As it's her first time in foal, Doug wanted me to check her over. Flotsam, do you remember her? She used to be a favourite of yours, I think. She's had modest wins, but her owner thought she might do better in the breeding stakes. As I was here, I couldn't let my favourite sister arrive to the dour face of old Gibson, could I?"

"I'm your only sister," she pointed out. "Why are you really here?" *As if she didn't know.*

Rick turned to Jack and held out his hand. "Richard Brown. Middle brother."

Jack shook hands affably. "Pleased to meet you. Jack Sinclair. Also a middle brother. Not ideal, is it? You get caught for all the awkward tasks. Checking on unknown fiancés, for example."

Rick raised his eyebrows at his sister. "You didn't mention he was smart."

"It ought to have been a foregone conclusion," she replied. "Why else would I have said yes?"

"Can't say I'm not relieved. Hop in. It's just you two. Aidan arrived earlier." He glanced at Jack. "Our younger brother. Studying at Barts."

Lucy pulled herself up to the seat, frowning. "Aidan's here? Why? It can't be to see me or to meet Jack. He could do that in London if he wasn't so busy."

"Am I his confidant? Ask him yourself if you can get close enough." He clicked his tongue. "Walk on, Duchess. Let's get the prodigal back for lunch."

He's worried about Aidan. Lucy felt a twinge of guilt about not pushing her younger brother harder for a visit. But he was twenty-two, old enough not to need a nursemaid, and Lucy had hated well-meaning interference at that age. Or any age.

At home, Jack charmed her mother in under a minute. Her father cast him a shrewd glance the same way he sized up an unknown racehorse, then nodded to the company and left for the course.

"You're honoured," said her mother. "He wouldn't have come in at all if it wasn't for you only being here for a few hours."

Lucy reminded herself how fond she was of her family. "Can't be helped. I got today off as a favour because I told the office my father had a horse running in the big race. We'll come for a weekend another time."

Her mother sniffed and turned to quiz Aidan on the young lady one of her acquaintances had seen him with in town. "I could hardly say I didn't know who the girl was when she asked. I just said you'd always been popular with the crowd."

"Simply a friend, Mother."

"I hope you aren't taking her about, spending your allowance and distracting yourself from your studies. You've still got another year until you qualify."

"I'm not likely to forget," said Aidan.

"You never talk about how it's going."

"I should think I don't, considering I was in theatre all day yesterday. Wouldn't want to put everyone off their lunch." He pushed back his chair and smiled. "Which was delicious as usual. Who's for the races? Will we all fit in one trap?"

Yes, thought Lucy, definitely something not right.

Jack found himself in the second pony trap with Lucy and her sisters-in-law. They were pleasant women, but older than Lucy and wrapped up in their husbands and families. After admiring her engagement ring and mentally pricing her new London suit, they returned to each other's company and conversation.

Jack was no stranger to the Rowley Mile, though seeing the other side of the sport was new to him. There was business in the air, a watchful, serious feel to the people around them. He got out his race card, preparing to lay a judicious selection of bets and keep his ears and eyes open. Aidan Brown was doing the same, a wrinkle of calculation on his brow. Some five years younger than his sister, he had a thin, clever face and the same gleam of humour that characterised Lucy and Rick. Jack rather thought he would make an excellent doctor.

The big race today was the Cambridgeshire Handicap. "Does your father train any of these?" he asked Lucy, tapping the list.

"Yes, but there are twenty-one runners, so it's a fearful free-for-all. Choose the favourite and a long shot if you want to hedge your bets. I quite like the look of Medal for the Cambridgeshire. I remember him winning as a two-year-old last year. Put five shillings on for me, can you?"

Jack went to place their bets. Aidan was just in front of him. Hedging bets must be a family strategy. Aidan's money was being carefully laid out where he was hoping it might do the most good. "And lastly, two pounds each on Medal and Niantic for the Cambridgeshire," he said.

Jack did a rapid calculation. Twenty pounds in all. That was a lot for an impoverished medical student.

When he mentioned it to Lucy, she nibbled her lip worriedly. "A few shillings is usually his limit. What sort of trouble has he got himself into?"

"Ask him."

"I intend to. Whether he gives me a straight answer is another matter."

They watched the races amidst the family and a number of their friends. There were nods of approval when a 'trained by Harry Brown' horse did well, grunts when a different yard ran out the winner. One particular voice forced itself on Jack's ear.

"Do you know that gentleman?" he asked Lucy, indicating a man wearing a loud overcoat and giving an even louder laugh.

Lucy glanced at the group around her eldest brother. "In the dark red check? Basil Milcombe. One of my father's owners. He had a winner earlier and he's also got mares in foal with Douglas. Why?"

Many reasons, none of them good. "I know him of old. I've never much liked the company he keeps."

"Doesn't surprise me. I always give him a wide berth. He's fanatical about horses and very informed when it comes to laying bets. He's a real club man, bores on forever about form and betting odds. Nothing else exists."

As the Cambridgeshire Handicap approached, more people jostled for a position where they could see the race. Jack carefully allowed a number of them to come between him and Basil Milcombe.

"Nine furlongs," he commented. "Odd length."

Lucy nodded. "It's the Rowley Mile, plus a furlong. That's what the original sponsor wanted. Did you know there were seventeen different courses a hundred years ago, all made up from bits and pieces of the main ones we have now?"

"Really?"

"Yes, the spectators probably spent more time moving between the different start and finish posts than they did watching the actual races. Most of them were on horseback too in those days. It must have been bedlam."

"They're off," called someone.

Jack saw Aidan grow tense. As with the previous races, they heard the hoof beats before they saw anything. When the horses surged into sight, a tight pack was clearly in advance of the rest.

"Medal's going to take it," said Milcombe confidently.

"No, it's Niantic." That was Aidan, his voice rising in excitement. "Look at him go."

"At odds of twenty-five to one? Some hope."

A confusion of horseflesh, crouched jockeys and flying hooves thundered past.

"Good God," said Douglas, astonishment in his voice. "I do believe it's a dead heat. Medal and Niantic crossing the line together. How often does that happen!"

Aidan swallowed, obviously sick with disappointment. "Once too many. All the same..." A frantic look of calculation shuttered his face.

Lucy turned to Jack, amused. "They both came first and they both came second. I fancy only the bookmakers are going to be pleased by that."

Aidan certainly wasn't, thought Jack, as the young man turned away. Why did he need money so badly? "If you ask me, you need to talk to your brother sooner rather than later," he said.

Lucy gave a businesslike nod. "I will. My mother always puts on a spread on the last day of a meeting. He won't miss that."

Nor did anyone else. Large gatherings were nothing new to Jack, but the crowded reception rooms in the family home made private talk impossible.

"Where's Aidan?" Lucy asked, once people had thinned out a little. "We're off soon. He can travel back with us."

"Gone," replied Douglas. "Milcombe offered him a lift. Jolly good of him, putting himself out for a pup. I expected him to come back with me for another look at

Flotsam. Still, Rick was optimistic about her, so I daresay that put his mind at rest."

"More than mine is," muttered Lucy to Jack. "I'll have to write to him now and have him ignore the letter as usual. Let's say our goodbyes."

In the train, Jack put his hat on the seat and stretched. "I enjoyed today. Did I pass muster?"

She snuggled against him. "Can you doubt it? I only hope I do as well when I meet your parents."

Her tone was preoccupied. Jack dropped a kiss on her forehead. "Aidan is twenty-two. A grown man in the eyes of the world. What can you do?"

Lucy made a cross noise. "Nothing. Wait for him to reply to my letter. I wish he hadn't gone off with Basil Milcombe. He's not a good influence."

Jack was inclined to agree. He found his priorities for tomorrow had changed. Milcombe would bear a little light investigation.

CHAPTER TWO

Paul Kent Architects was located in a tall Georgian terrace in Fitzroy Square. Lucy walked up the two shallow steps to the front door, thinking what a shame so many houses of this type were now used for commerce. Soulless businesses rather than laughter-filled family homes. A voice in her head pointed out that even if she wasn't quite the working girl she was pretending to be, she would have to sell an awful lot of books before she and Jack could contemplate living somewhere like this.

In the hallway, cream walls set off framed prints of design projects. On her right was the open door leading to the reception area where a superior young woman greeted clients and answered the telephone. Lucy and the other typists worked out of sight in the room behind. To the left of the front door was Mr Kent's room. A century ago it had been the library, and it still retained the original fittings and grandeur. Any client invited in to discuss their requirements couldn't fail to be reassured that Paul Kent was the perfect man to tackle their project.

Lucy nodded to the receptionist and went down the hallway to the typists' room. "Good morning, Miss Reed," she said to the senior typist as she crossed to the stand to hang up her coat.

Miss Reed peered over her spectacles. She was tall and thin, had a fearsome shorthand speed and, Lucy suspected, harboured a blameless passion for Mr Kent. "Good morning, Miss Brown. Did you have an enjoyable day yesterday?"

"Yes, thank you. Very busy, with the racing first and then helping Mother with the evening meal, but so nice to see everyone."

Miss Reed gave an approving nod. Lucy mentally apologised to her mother for cavalierly making away with Cook and the kitchen maids.

"Did you back any winners?" That was little Miss Hodge, her face lively with interest.

"I did. Wasn't I lucky? One of my father's horses came in first." She addressed Miss Reed deferentially. "I took the liberty of stopping at the ABC and buying us each a cream bun for elevenses to celebrate. If you are agreeable, that is?"

"Ooh, I love a cream bun," said Miss Hodge. "What a dear you are."

"I should have thought," said Miss Reed repressively, "you would be saving any windfalls of that nature to go towards your marriage."

Really, the woman was a killjoy. "Oh I am," said Lucy, "but it was four buns for the price of three at the ABC, and as there are four of us, I didn't think it would hurt." She hung her hat on a peg, hoping she looked suitably crestfallen.

Miss Reed inclined her head. "It was a generous thought and will make a nice treat. Betting is not something I am in favour of, but as it was a horse your father had trained, I daresay you were obliged to."

"There's nothing wrong with a small flutter, Miss Reed," said Miss Hodge. "Dad won two pounds at the greyhound track last week."

"Each to his own, Miss Hodge. Gambling is a very chancy affair and has led to many a downfall. I prefer to rely on my own small investments. There is nothing risky about them. Each of my ten pound units in Consolidated Cocoa pays twelve shillings a quarter and has done for the past three years."

Lucy turned around, open-mouthed. Even quiet Mrs Corrigan, typing a proposal at her corner desk, looked up briefly in amazement.

"But that's a twenty-four percent return each year," said Lucy, dazedly doing the sums in her head. "That's... that's astonishing."

"It's because the director puts everyone's units together so he can buy at a discount. And of course I've still got my original stake to redeem whenever I want."

It had to be a trick. Nothing made twenty-four percent these days. "You were lucky to find such an opportunity," said Lucy.

"Indeed, and any time I want to buy another unit, I can."

"Only if you have ten pounds to spare," murmured Mrs Corrigan.

Lucy sent her a sympathetic glance. With two young children and an invalid husband, every penny had to earn its keep in Mrs Corrigan's household.

"My weekly pay is always gone by Wednesday, what with rent and meals," declared Miss Hodge. "I do keep two bob for the dance hall on a Saturday. It seems a lot, but the band is awfully good and the dancing goes on until midnight."

"If you stopped smoking, you could put those pennies aside and give them to Mr Trelawny when you had enough for a unit share," pointed out Miss Reed.

Miss Hodge looked appalled. "It would take years. I'd rather smoke."

Trelawny. Lucy made a mental note of the name. As Jack often said, when something sounded too good to be true, it usually was. "Twelve shillings a quarter, though," she said. "That would buy a fair number of gaspers. Was it an advertisement in one of the financial columns that put you on to it, Miss Reed?"

"A client of Mr Kent was talking about his own investments and mentioned the opportunity to buy some units. He gave me Mr Trelawny's address and suggested I enquire."

Lucy sat down and uncovered her typewriter. *Don't get involved, Lucy. That's not what you are here for.* It couldn't hurt though, surely? Detecting was more fun than typing measurements and quotes and lists of materials.

Sadly, this job was proving rather a disappointment in that respect. She was used to taking temporary work in various spheres, soaking up the atmosphere and finding out what went into particular careers, then using the experience as settings for her books. She'd been hopeful during her first week when Mr Koivisto, who looked more like a matinee idol than a senior draughtsman, had seen her in the hall studying a framed design for a modern kitchen. He had raised an enquiring eyebrow and she'd said it was beautiful, but impractical in a slip of a kitchenette like hers.

Mr Koivisto's ensuing ten minute treatise on looking beyond conventional boundaries, along with practical considerations about recognising load-bearing walls and the design potential of plywood, had held the excitement she'd been looking for. Since then however, the only insights had come from the brief few minutes she spent taking tea into the draughtsmen's office. It was nothing like enough to write *Anna Adams: Trainee Architect* or *The Gable End Murders.* That would teach her to go answering adverts in a fit of pique. A waste of a month that she could have spent writing something she *did* know about.

Making the tea was traditionally the task of the most junior typist. With the unfortunate Miss Smith now convalescing after her emergency appendix operation, it fell to Lucy. This morning she had the kettle boiling, the teapots for upstairs and downstairs warming and the trays of cups ready. She poured milk into the various jugs, added the sugar bowls and spoons and tipped the cream buns out of their paper bag on to a plate for the typists' room.

"You're frightfully good at this," said Miss Hodge, lured by the promise of the buns into helping carry the various trays from the kitchen to their respective destinations. "Better than Smithy. Much better than me."

Lucy didn't mention that four weeks of making early morning tea for a floor of guests at the Bay Sands Hotel had considerably honed her hospitality skills. "There are always a lot of people to make tea for at my father's stables."

"You're so lucky. It must be even more exciting than greyhound racing. And greyhound racing *is* all right, whatever Miss Reed says, because I saw Mr Kent himself at the White City track on Monday when I was there with Dad. A horse racing stable sounds lovely."

"It isn't," said Lucy. "The day starts far too early and because he is my father, he considers I should help out for free. Why do you think I'm here instead?"

Miss Hodge giggled and took the receptionist's tray through, ready for that damsel to deliver Mr Kent's tea personally. Lucy put the typists' tea on their side table and was about to return for the upstairs tray when Mr Kent walked into the room.

It was universally acknowledged that Paul Kent was the personality behind the practice. With his easy manner, classic looks and bonhomie, he charmed clients and staff alike. Lucy, who had met a number of good-looking gentlemen over the years and had failed to be bowled over by any of them, was unconvinced.

Mr Kent smiled around the room with deprecating whimsy. "Miss Reed, I wonder if you could find me the Ingram portfolio before Mrs Ingram arrives. I'd do it myself, but I can never understand your system. After your tea, of course, no need to hurry. Oh, cream buns, very nice." He plucked one off the plate and walked out, eating it.

"Well, really," said Miss Hodge in outrage once the door was safely closed. "I bet he smelled them. He could just as easily have rung through for the file like he usually does."

It was clear Miss Reed was mortified by this cavalier behaviour from her favourite. "He wouldn't have realised they were only for us," she said with a painful smile. "It doesn't matter. I can do very well without a bun."

"Oh, it happens all the time at home," said Lucy cheerfully. She quickly cut each bun into four. "There, three quarters each. Save mine for me. I must get the other tray upstairs before the tea goes cold."

"Mr Koivisto is so absent-minded he wouldn't notice," said Miss Hodge. "I was taking a letter the other day and he just stopped mid-sentence, then dashed over to his board and started drawing a design for a new chair."

Maybe he wouldn't, thought Lucy as she closed the door on Miss Reed's remonstration for impertinence, but Miss Kent certainly would. Lucy hadn't been here three days before she realised Paul Kent was too busy wining and dining clients to take an active part in the designs going out under his name. All the real work was done by his sister.

Christina Kent was the epitome of the modern working woman. The opinion in the typists' room was that Mr Koivisto was sweet on her, and Lucy could see why. In her early forties, a little older than her brother, she was fine-drawn and slender, with excellent bones and a shining cap of dark hair. She was also punctiliously polite, making a point of coming down on Lucy's first morning and saying a few words welcoming her to the firm, even though it would only be of short duration while Miss Smith recovered from her operation.

It had made Lucy feel shabby for being there under false pretences. She had hopes of asking Miss Kent about what it took to become a female architect, but how to do it was a puzzle she had yet to solve. Temporary typists did not hobnob with the management.

She juggled the handle to the draughtsmen's office with her elbow and put the tray on the table by the wall. She then poured Miss Kent's tea and carried it across the passage, knocking at the door before going in.

Christina Kent's room must have been the main salon in Regency times. High-ceilinged and elegant, it was painted the palest lemon, the curtain swags a rich gold. The furniture was modern, all clean lines and curves in beech-veneered plywood. Geometric designs incised into the panels of the bench seats matched those on the tall cupboards at the far end of the room. A drawing board stood in front of one set of windows. The large table in the centre of the room was strewn with papers and models. As ever, Lucy smiled with involuntary delight when she entered. "Your tea, Miss Kent."

"Thank you." The older woman looked quizzically at her expression.

"This is simply the most beautiful room," said Lucy, blushing. "I think so every time I come in here. It's so clever the way it is traditional and modern at the same time."

Miss Kent laughed. "I am glad you like it. The key to renovating old rooms is to make them work for you without destroying their character. This room has always been used for living in. One can modernise, but only with a purpose, and the purpose has to fit the use of the room. For me, that is living and working, even though I live in this room in a very different way from the original occupants." She smiled at Lucy's bewildered face. "Never mind. You like my room, because it is fit for the purpose I put it to. That is, in essence, what I am saying."

This was what Lucy was thirsty for. The rationale behind architectural decisions. "I... I thought you had a flat upstairs," she said, desperate to keep Miss Kent talking.

"I do, but when I am involved with a project, it occupies more than traditional office hours. This room is my working space, it contains my inspiration, my soul. I am frequently here the whole evening before going upstairs to bed."

"Oh," said Lucy. "That explains why it feels so much richer and fuller than other offices I've worked in. Thank you. That's so interesting,"

"Richer and fuller?" Miss Kent considered the phrase. "The cupboards are full of paperwork, of course, but you are right that the room is rich with ideas. When I sit at my table I am reminded of all the designs I have ever done. When I walk around I remember other problems I have solved pacing these rugs." She picked up her cup and took a sip. "Forgive me, I am keeping you from your break."

That was a hint if ever Lucy had heard one. "Oh no, I find it fascinating." She had turned the handle to leave when the door opened, making her jump.

Mr Koivisto took a few quick steps into the room. "I beg your pardon," he said to Lucy. "I startled you. Christina, do you have the preliminary sketches we did for the Ingram project? Paul is asking for the designs."

Miss Kent crossed to the curving bench seat running around the corner of the room and touched a panel underneath it. A cleverly concealed cupboard sprang open. "Is that on again? I thought Mrs Ingram had decided against it."

Vilho Koivisto shrugged. "You know Paul. He hopes to persuade her into signing."

"A waste of his time. She will change her mind again next week. She is a very stupid woman."

She handed him the folder and in return he sent her a look full of amusement. "A stupid woman with a great deal of money. This is what attracts Paul." He hurried out with an absent thank you to Lucy who still held the door.

She shut it quickly and went downstairs, hoping Miss Kent would not think she'd been deliberately eavesdropping. With any luck, she could capitalise on today's promising chat and talk to her some more. It wouldn't do to offend her.

The nameplate on the plain, unremarkable door read 'Chief Inspector Curtis'. Jack knocked and went in. The sandy-haired man at the desk also seemed plain and unremarkable until he looked up and Jack met his keen stare.

"Morning, Uncle Bob. Not busy arresting anyone?"

"I *had* scheduled myself half-an-hour to read through reports. How did yesterday go? Get on with the family? Back any winners?"

"Yes to both, but that's not why I dropped in. I ran across an acquaintance of ours at Newmarket."

Curtis sat back in his chair. "Go on."

"Basil Milcombe."

"And?"

"And I wondered what he was up to these days, because Lucy's younger brother seems to be in a spot of bother, but before she could find out the problem, Milcombe had offered him a ride home to London and whisked him away. The general feeling was that it was out of character. Milcombe has horses with Lucy's father, mares with her older brother and I gather he is usually the life and soul of the party on race days, talking horseflesh and betting odds until the small hours. Even more so when he's had a good win, which he did yesterday."

"Leaving early wasn't simply an excuse on his part to avoid you?"

Jack shook his head. "He's never given any indication that he suspected my involvement in getting his Guildford gambling den closed down."

"At his old game then? Using vulnerable greenhorns as dupes to add to his own coffers? Does the boy have money?"

"Far from it. He's a medical student at Barts. Still got a year to go."

"It wouldn't bother Milcombe if he ruined the lad, family friend or not. I'll ask Maynard to put someone on to checking his movements. If you can find out what's biting young Brown it might give us a lead. Meanwhile, what are you and your young lady doing tonight?"

Jack grinned. "I imagine you are about to tell me."

"The Black Cat club in Frith Street. Been there?"

"Not yet. There are only so many Soho haunts I can visit in one night. That's quite a new one, isn't it? Does it have something extra to recommend it?"

"That's what I'd like to know. As with all these places, the owners are hidden behind company names. However, the licensee is one Youssif Arama, an Algerian gentleman last seen presiding over the dying rites of the Splendour."

"I remember. The club with the elastic interpretation of licensing laws."

"Aren't they all when they can get away with it? The intriguing point about the Black Cat is that the banker behind it is our friend George Forrest."

Jack stared. "Now that *is* interesting. I wouldn't have thought him the type. Aside from bankers not generally viewing nightclubs as profitable investments, Forrest has a name for being moral and upright. As sharp as a razor at the bridge table, but with the conversation of an early Victorian patriarch. It makes it all the more strange that he tolerates Edward Carter."

"I daresay he finds the association with a tobacco millionaire worth his while," said his uncle drily.

"True. All those Forrest saplings to feed. Perhaps being on the board of Carter's Bay Sands Hotel has given him a taste for the hospitality business. Funnily enough, I have heard the name mentioned recently."

"More of your circle going there now we've closed down the Forty Three again, probably."

"Very likely. Society is a restless beast. You'd like me to become one of the new faithful and to keep my eyes and ears open?"

"You and Lucy. A fashionable young couple out for a good time. It's a hunch, which policemen are not supposed to regard, but the combination of Arama and Forrest arouses my curiosity. As soon as we have grounds for thinking something illegal might be going on, we can apply to see the records."

"Or even get a warrant. Right you are. I'll join as a member this evening. Ease myself in gradually and start putting out feelers."

CHAPTER THREE

The morning wore on. At twelve, Miss Reed and Miss Hodge departed for lunch. Lucy glanced over to where Mrs Corrigan was typing. Horrified, she saw a tear on her cheek and rushed into speech. "I don't want to interfere, but you look very unhappy. Is something wrong?"

The woman looked up, her eyes swimming. "The landlord came yesterday for his rent. He's putting it up by another two shillings from next week and it's high enough already. Alfred thinks he wants to evict us and get another family in our rooms. I don't know how we are going to manage. I can't stop thinking about it."

The plea cut Lucy to the heart. She jumped up and ran across the room to give Mrs Corrigan a hug. "Oh, you poor thing. How mean of your landlord. And there was me so pleased with my win that I spent it on buns." She darted back for her handbag and opened her purse. "Here, I've still got five bob of it left. Put it towards the next two weeks' rent and a bit for the week after. I couldn't spend it now, honestly I couldn't, not knowing you need it."

Mrs Corrigan stared at the two half-crowns Lucy held out. "Oh, Miss Brown, I can't."

Lucy put the coins in her hand and folded her fingers over them. "Yes, you can. No one will know. It's not charity,

I didn't earn it. I had a bit of luck and you could do with it. Is it worth asking Miss Kent if she has any extra work you could take on?"

"I... I could. I hadn't thought. I have wondered about looking for other places with more pay, but all I can do is type. I never expected to be still working once I was married. All I ever wanted was a little house to keep clean and a family to cook and mend for. Now Alfred has to mind the children while I go out to earn. He says at least he's here with me and the kiddies, not six feet under in a French field, but it is hard when I remember how he used to be. He can't even get much fresh air where we are now. He'd like a bit of garden really. Used to grow lovely veg before the war. Now his nerves are in pieces and he gets so tired. My sister says to go to the coast for the day on an excursion." She looked at Lucy in despair. "I ask you, all that way on a charabanc? And what are we to pay with? She just doesn't think."

"The war shook everything up," said Lucy sombrely. "I was an auxiliary nurse. I saw the men who came back, the ones who needed our convalescent home. The waste of those lives makes me angry still."

Mrs Corrigan gave a bitter laugh. "People say he should be proud of being brave and doing his duty to the country. Alfred says he wasn't particularly brave. He went where they told him to go, sat in the trenches until they said to fight, and got gassed for believing the officers knew what they were doing."

Lucy nodded. "My cousin died in France. We were told the country was grateful. We didn't want gratitude. We wanted Henry back."

"Grateful. Not so grateful it can't give Alfred more than a little bitty pension to try to live on." She dabbed at her eyes. "I'm sorry, sometimes it just gets too much. I feel better now. Isn't that daft?"

Lucy gave the other woman's hand a squeeze and went back to her own table. "It doesn't do to bottle things up. Do you want to share a pot of tea when it's our turn for lunch?"

Mrs Corrigan shook her head. "It's kind, but Alfred will have mine ready. It's nice to have time alone with him in the middle of the day."

After leaving his uncle to get on with the work of Scotland Yard, Jack considered which gentlemen's club would best serve his purpose for a rubber of bridge and a spot of lunch. He wasn't a member of the Jockey Club, that being reserved for racehorse owners. He *was* a member of the Turf Club, but so was Milcombe and he didn't want to get quite that close to him this soon.

He settled on the Bath Club in Dover Street which was a favourite amongst his sporting acquaintance. A discussion of yesterday's racing at Newmarket would be entirely natural and should enable him to bring up the subject of Milcombe and his current activities without suspicion. Idle gossip often provided useful topics for investigation.

Jack strolled into the coffee lounge. It was early, but he could get on with his daily tasks while he waited. He ordered coffee and leafed through the newspapers provided for patrons. An advertisement in one of the personal columns caught his eye. *'Ebony kitten wants happy and comfortable Saturday night'*, but with no box number or contact details.

Jack whistled soundlessly. It looked as though Uncle Bob's instincts had been correct. He made a note and had identified another three bogus messages by the time enough gentlemen had appeared to make conversation the order of the day rather than reading advertisements and writing naive enquiries to box numbers.

"Where have you been hiding yourself, Sinclair? Changed your haunts? Saw the announcement of your impending nuptials in *The Times*."

Jack surveyed Viscounts Nicholson and Jarmaine over the top of his newspaper before folding it and casting it on a side table. "Here and there, Theo. I was at Newmarket yesterday for the Cambridgeshire Handicap. Dead heat. Oddest thing you ever saw."

Theo's expression became nostalgic. "Something rather fine about the turf. We were considering buying a racehorse at one time, weren't we, Hubert? Seems to be no end of work involved though, and even once you've bought it, there's no guarantee the nag will win."

"If there was, the bookmakers would all go out of business," pointed out Jack.

His friends pondered this. "No bad thing," said Hubert Jarmaine. "Most of them are thieves and robbers. Can't buy a horse now. Not with the wedding coming up. Amanda would take a pretty dim view of half a racehorse as a wedding present."

Theo nodded owlishly. "You're right. Even if we called it Jumanda or Amalie."

Jack bit the insides of his cheeks to keep a straight face. "Conventional creatures, ladies. You're safer sticking to the traditional diamond parure. It's only confirmed bachelors like Basil Milcombe who can afford racehorses. He was at Newmarket giving the benefit of his wisdom to anyone within hearing distance."

"Him," said Theo. "He was in here the other week boasting about how he gets seventy guineas a pop whenever one of his stallions covers a mare. I wouldn't be a horse. Fancy being expected to perform to order."

"Shocking," agreed Jack. "It must work though. He always has money to flash about."

"He has investments," said Hubert gloomily. "He asked

about mine and said he could put me on to a good thing if I was interested, but I told him all my capital is tied up with the trustees."

"Good thing too," said Theo. "Wouldn't trust Milcombe. He's like one of those bounders in shows who seem like regular chaps until you find out at the end he's been after the hero's girl all along."

It was odd, thought Jack, how surprisingly often Theo came up with wayward insights like this.

"Took the girls to a topping show last night," his friend continued. "It had that fellow as the comic butler who was the grandfather in that show a while back about the Irish girl who pretends to get a divorce so she can remarry the comic fellow's grandson. Saw it at the Hippodrome, didn't we, Hubert?"

Jack disentangled this. "Can you possibly mean *Mercenary Mary*?"

"That's the one," said Theo, looking pleased. "Knew you'd know it. Beats me how you remember these things."

"It beats me how you persuaded Julie to marry you," replied Jack.

"I told her I loved her. Think I always will."

Hubert stirred. "Better have our swim before lunch. You can be our witness, Jack. We told ma-in-law-to-be there was a competition on. She was all for us going for another blasted fitting. I said to pa-in-law-to-be, one morning suit is much like any other. No point buying new. My man will see to it I look presentable."

"Did it work?" asked Jack, interested.

"No. Mrs Lester fixed us with that look she has and decreed Theo and I must both have new togs for the ceremony. Did you hear about the reception? She's only persuaded Theo's batty cousin to lend us the moated manor for the wedding party. Wants to go one better than Veronique Carter's marriage to the Earl of Elvedon."

"Tell you what," said his friend with an air of discovery. "I'll be glad once the wedding is over and we've got the girls to ourselves."

"I believe you," said Hubert. "Word of advice, Jack. Break off your engagement now, before you get tangled up with mothers-in-law, new suits and diamond necklaces."

"No danger of that," said Jack cheerfully. "Lucy will be perfectly happy with a racehorse. Her father trains them."

Lucy had been charmed when Jack met her from work, saying she deserved to be taken out to dinner and suggesting she wear the orange dancing dress she'd bought in New York so they could go on somewhere after they'd eaten.

Now she looked sideways at him, sauntering along in his evening clothes with the unconscious ease of one who'd been accustomed to starched shirt-fronts since the cradle, and said, "Are you going to enlighten me as to why we are going to the Black Cat club?"

"Latest place. Jack Sinclair is always seen at the latest place. Cocktails and a floor show, a decent band and dancing. What could be nicer?"

"Nicer would be not having to be up early tomorrow to go to work. Architectural documents require concentration at the best of times. It could be a very expensive mistake if I mistype dimensions and quantities while half asleep. Why are we really going to this place? What are we looking for?"

Jack tucked her arm inside his. "Why do nightclubs exist?"

"To give your set pleasure," she said promptly. "To provide the bands and the dancers with a living."

"That's what they *do*, that's not why they exist. They exist to make money. The backer behind the Black Cat, for example, would have looked only at the financial prospects before investing. He's not concerned about alleviating the boredom of rich people with time on their hands. He doesn't give two hoots about ensuring a jazz band and a troupe of dancers don't go hungry this season. He wants to make his money back and then some."

"He's going to be upset when he finds out nightclubs go bust all the time," observed Lucy.

"They rarely fold until they've provided a profit for the shareholders. Short term investment. Make the money and move on. The interesting thing in this case is that the manager has a history of shady practices and the backer is George Forrest."

Lucy absorbed this. "The same Mr Forrest who is involved with Mr Carter and the Bay Sands Hotel?"

"The very same. We are here to observe. If the club is genuine, establishing ourselves as regular visitors means when the tide of popularity turns and the club starts bending the rules in order to hold on to their clientele, they won't worry about me sitting at my normal table taking it all in. So tonight we smile, chatter, dance and keep our eyes open."

"Easy. Why is it the latest hot spot? What makes it more attractive than the others?"

Jack shrugged. "Why is anything ever? Better quality food? Louder band? Nightclubs are transient places. Something tickles the fancy of somebody with a wide circle of friends and for a few weeks the club rakes in the profits. Then the scene shifts to somewhere with cheaper drinks and a hotter floor show and that's when the inducements to clients become borderline illegal."

"It doesn't sound like a wholesome environment for a career-girl book," said Lucy regretfully.

"*Sadie Stevens: Showgirl?* Your publisher would have a conniption fit. And call me old-fashioned, but I'm not much taken with the idea of you getting a part-time job there just to soak up the requisite knowledge to write it."

She patted his arm. "Too sweet."

The Black Cat club was discovered crammed between a chophouse and a twenty-four hour tailoring outfit. From within came the insistent pulse of a jazz band. The black cat on the sign eyed them enigmatically over its shoulder.

"Good evening," said Jack to the uniformed commissionaire. "The club is open for membership, I take it?"

The commissionaire swept a practised eye over Jack's impeccable tailoring. "That's right, sir. Box office on the right. Cloakroom on the left. Thank you, sir," he added, sliding his gloved hand momentarily into his pocket.

While Jack dealt with the formalities, Lucy left her wrap in the cloakroom along with his overcoat. She was aware, as he turned to join her, that they were being observed with detached interest by the swarthy type in the box office. "I like the decor," she said in a suitably bubbly voice. "Divine colour. Matches my dress."

Jack made an enthusiastic grab for her hand. "I'd better keep hold of you in case I lose you amongst the wall hangings."

They both laughed as if they'd said something terribly amusing and, following the sound of the music, descended from the burnt orange, silk-draped foyer down a flight of gilded steps into the club itself.

There was a bar at the bottom of the staircase with a steel counter and bottles winking seductively on the shelves.

Jack's eyebrows rose. "Look at that," he murmured. "They are advertising cold lager. Now that *is* a declaration of a classy establishment if it's the real thing. Continental, lighter than beer, three times the price."

They continued down the stairs. A smiling waiter

ushered them into a gold, cinnamon and turquoise room, with cleverly-lit slim box pillars and a ceiling that disappeared into dappled grey. Vivacious groups already half-filled the tables set around a large dance floor. Wall lamps glowed in the semi-circular booths lining two of the walls. Tobacco smoke wreathed in the air. A seven-piece band blasted the latest rhythms from a raised dais in one corner.

Lucy and Jack were shown to a small round table towards the back of the room. The waiter didn't turn a hair when Lucy said she'd prefer lager to a cocktail. He was back with their drinks almost before they'd settled themselves down.

"Your uncle has his facts wrong. This cannot be the latest place," said Lucy presently.

Jack looked at her, amused. "Why not?"

"Because we have been here for at least five minutes and not a single person you know has come over to slap you on the back and comment about what a small world it is."

"Just you wait. Where Jack Sinclair leads, others will follow. It's early yet. It will fill up in an hour or so."

"I did mention I had work tomorrow, yes?"

"Fear not, Cinderella, tonight is simply to establish ourselves. We stay for a bit, dance for a bit, leave reluctantly and are drawn back tomorrow. Very much the sort of clients nightclub proprietors love. Meanwhile, judging by the way the musicians have just brought themselves to a conclusion, I imagine the floor show is about to start. Prepare to look enthusiastic."

As it happened, Lucy didn't need to pretend. The cabaret number was surprisingly slick and polished. The dancers wore strapless, diamond-patterned harlequin suits which would have been dazzling enough even without the fast, synchronised twirls and leaps that still kept them miraculously inside the dance floor.

"That's one reason for this being the latest place right there," murmured Jack, leaning back to keep all the dancers in view.

Lucy agreed. She couldn't believe a number of the customers were ignoring the routine, continuing to smoke, drink, eat slivers of ham and talk over the music.

"It's as good as anything you'd find in the West End," continued Jack. "One wonders why the troupe is here and not on the stage of the Lyceum."

"Better pay, probably. Or a nicer sprung floor."

"It could be. There's certainly been a lot of money expended in setting it up." He nodded towards the dais. "That's the Harry Bidgood Band. I've heard them at hotel dances. You don't get well-known musicians for nothing. The question is, why go to this much trouble just for a nightclub?"

"How are you going to find out?"

"Sometimes it's simply a case of putting all the small things together and seeing if they add up to anything. Bravo!" He applauded loudly as the dance routine finished. A dancer at the end of the row, with sleek red hair and a more liberal use of make-up than the others, looked across alertly, then away again as she took in Lucy sitting next to him.

"I do hope I'm not cramping your style," said Lucy.

He grinned. "Never. Shall we dance?"

After an energetic quickstep followed by an equally lively Charleston, they returned to the table. "It seems to have got busier," said Lucy.

"As I predicted. Look, Tufty Thomas and a group of pals are being shown to a table over there. Not all the extra people are customers. The redhead sashaying across from the bar, for instance."

Lucy looked closer. "She's the leader of the dance troupe. The one who had her eye on you. Now wearing a cocktail dress. Several of the others are hovering by the bar. Oh..."

Jack quirked an eyebrow at her. "Oh?"

Lucy edged her chair backwards into the cinnamon-turquoise shadows by the pillar. "This could be tricky."

"You're as bad as talking to Theo."

Lucy kicked him indignantly. "Do you see the gentleman in the third booth? The one waving a ten shilling note at your redhead."

"Successfully, it seems."

"That is my employer, Mr Paul Kent. Last seen helping himself to Miss Reed's cream bun." She watched covertly as the redheaded dancer undulated into the booth and sat very close to Mr Kent, smiling up into his face. He stubbed out his cigarette and slid his hand over her silk-stockinged leg. The dancer's smile became as knowing as the one on the painted cat outside.

Jack took a pull at his lager. "He's got his eyes on more than a cream bun now. This is the Mr Kent with a wife, three children and a house in St John's Wood, is it?"

"That's him," said Lucy.

"Awkward."

"Ho, Sinclair! This is a jolly place, isn't it?"

Jack sighed inaudibly. "Evening, Tufty. It seems to be, yes. We thought we'd try it out. Can't remember who told me about it now."

"Elvedon mentioned it in the club this morning. I wouldn't let that sway me - being Elvedon, you know - but as well as going on about the decor being a cut above the usual places, he said the dance routines were quite something. The waiter-jonnie says we've just missed one, but there's another in half-an-hour."

The young man was looking with open curiosity at Lucy as he spoke. He got out his cigarette case and glanced around for a light, putting it back again when he couldn't see any matches.

Jack said casually. "It will be worth the wait, judging by the last routine. Do you know Tufty Thomas, Lucy? Not a spark of talent at school, but now one of London's most enthusiastic cocktail connoisseurs. Tufty, this is my fiancée, Miss Brown. We are having an evening *à deux*."

Lucy suppressed a chuckle and smiled at Mr Thomas.

"That's a hint, isn't it? I can take a hint. Fancy you tying the knot at last. I didn't believe it when Jimmy Ward told me. Funny thing, I thought you looked familiar, Miss Brown, but it must have been someone else I was thinking of. See you around, I expect." He ambled back to his own party.

"Considering I was cleaning his room at the Bay Sands Hotel six weeks ago, I should think I do look familiar," said Lucy. "I see now why you weren't worried about taking me about in public."

Jack gave a short laugh. "Not all my friends are as unobservant as Tufty. Keep your eye on those booths. If one becomes free, we'll move into it. Then people will get used to seeing us together without feeling the need to interrogate me about it."

Because he was on a job here? Because he didn't want to draw attention to himself? Because she wasn't one of his set?

He smiled disarmingly, right into her eyes. "I don't want to share you."

"Liar," said Lucy, but her heart was warmed all the same. She glanced around the room to see if she recognised anyone else. And stiffened.

CHAPTER FOUR

"What is it?" asked Jack.

Lucy nodded towards the bar. "Fair girl in the yellow dress. I think she is one of the dancers. The man who was in the box office when we arrived has got his arm around her and is guiding her rather forcefully to sit with those two businessmen."

"So he is," said Jack in a grim tone. "That is Mr Youssif Arama, the manager, and this is definitely something the Yard will be interested in. Dancers joining gentlemen of their own free will for supper and conversation is one thing - as long as it goes no further actually on the premises. Coercion is something else."

"She's hating it, poor thing," said Lucy. "As soon as either of them lays so much as a finger on her, I'll be over there like lightning asking her to show me where the ladies' room is."

Jack nodded. "Good idea. She doesn't look old enough to be out on her own, does she? Oh, what's this...?"

There was an uneasy stir at the far end of the room as two gentlemen came down the stairs. The manager left the businessmen and moved swiftly across, his smile becoming very fixed as the newcomers took seats at the bar.

Jack sat back in his seat. "I doubt your rescue act will be needed. Watch."

Youssif Arama looked across the room and gave an infinitesimal upwards jerk of his head. The redheaded dancer in Mr Kent's booth let out a throaty laugh and was next seen unhurriedly crossing the floor, collecting the other dancers as she went. They disappeared through a side door hidden in the shadows.

"This is what comes of Mr Arama deserting his post in the box office," said Jack. "Evidently his assistant isn't as canny as he is."

"Sometimes," remarked Lucy, "you can be just a tiny bit irritating."

"Sorry. I believe the new revellers are representatives of the local police force, passing themselves off as members of the public and checking up in a friendly fashion on the proceedings."

"How can you tell?"

Jack smiled into her eyes, as if there was nothing on his mind but her. "They are making no attempt to blend in, they haven't brought partners, they are sitting at the bar not at one of the tables. Arama is no fool. There won't be anything untoward happening here for the rest of the night now."

As if to underline this, the businessmen finished their drinks and left, giving the gentlemen at the bar a wide berth.

"And don't come back," muttered Lucy.

The band played faster. More couples began to dance. Waiters became very busy circulating around the tables taking orders for food. Lucy looked across at Mr Kent's booth and discovered it was empty.

She nudged Jack. "Mr Kent has gone. Were you serious about taking a booth?"

"Gone? When? He didn't leave by the stairs."

"See for yourself."

Jack stood and took a few steps in that direction. He turned to her and made a beckoning gesture like an enamoured young gentleman in search of a bit of privacy. In the same spirit, she giggled, picked up her bag and their drinks and joined him, sliding around the curved, cushioned bench until she could see the room.

"Lucky for us, eh? Perhaps he didn't want to be spotted by anyone official with a lady who wasn't his wife," she said.

"Do you think so? He was hardly discreet in attracting her attention."

"He may have got carried away. These booths feel intimate once you are in them, but they aren't really. It's an illusion of velvet and dark wood." Lucy wrinkled her brow at the veneer panelling below the midnight-blue cushioned seat, wondering why it seemed familiar. She'd seen something similar quite recently. "Oh! These panels are decorated in the same way as the ones on the bench seats in Miss Kent's workroom. I wonder if Paul Kent Architects did the design of the club?"

Jack looked impressed. "That's a neat bit of deduction. It would explain how Kent knew of a side door to slip out of, in case the rozzers decided to take the names of the clients here tonight."

The geometric design really did seem exactly the same. Lucy dropped her hand and traced the incised pattern to the corner. Her fingers found a small cut-out notch. She pressed it and felt a concealed cupboard door spring open against her legs.

"What are you doing?" asked Jack.

She grinned at him. "Testing a theory. They *are* the same as Miss Kent's benches. She has cupboards under her seats too. I saw her open one this morning. It's such a clever, practical way of increasing storage space. Do you think if I ask nicely, they'd design me some for the flat? Mr Koivisto is very keen on plywood. He gets beautifully carried away when he talks about it."

Jack glanced swiftly at the hidden cupboard. "Ask him. Meanwhile you'd better close it again or the management are never going to let us come back." His voice changed suddenly. "Stop. Before you shut the panel, can you hide that gap? Pull your dress across or something?"

"This dress that is largely knee-length and comprised of velvet and satin streamers?"

"Damn. In that case, push the door nearly to, then slither away and I will slither seductively after you."

"Which could, after all, be why we wanted a booth."

"That's my girl."

She did as he suggested, sending him the sort of provocative look that would cause nobody any surprise to see him move closer to her. Indeed, she became so distracted by the sweet nothings he whispered in her ear that she barely noticed whatever it was he palmed from the cupboard. She did, however, hear the click as he closed it and let out a tiny shriek to cover the sound.

Jack's hand went to his pocket and back out again.

"Behave," she said clearly. "The next show is about to start. If it's as good as the first, I don't want to miss a single step."

The music came to a crashing stop. "Clear the floor, ladies and gentlemen," said the band leader, "and put your hands together for Miss Rose Garden and her Kitten Kaboodle."

This dance routine was, if anything, even better than the previous one. Lucy dropped her voice and murmured, "What did you find?"

Jack's voice was equally soft. "A small package, much like the packets of heroin I intercepted on the Atlantic Princess."

Drugs. An unpleasant chill went through Lucy. "Are you going to tell the police at the bar?"

"No."

"Why not?"

"Because I don't know if this is a single packet - someone's personal property - or if there is a whole cupboard full of the stuff. Once I tell the police, they are bound to act. I don't know enough to make the disruption of a police search worthwhile."

Lucy nodded. "And you don't want to be fingered as the one who caused it."

"It would certainly make future visits problematic."

"I can't even get a job here as a cleaner and check the other panels for concealed packets," she lamented. "My contract runs for the next two weeks."

"Sometimes, my love, you make my blood run cold. Not that it isn't a good idea. Uncle Bob could put someone in."

He really didn't want her working here. Lucy returned her attention to the dance routine, thinking hard.

"You are ominously quiet," said Jack.

"I was thinking I might ask tomorrow if Paul Kent Architects did the design. I could casually say I came tonight and the patterns looked familiar. I won't mention the concealed cupboard, but it would be nice to know."

"You don't fool me. You're wondering if Kent left the drugs here and disappeared before he could be searched, aren't you?"

"It's a possibility."

"There are any number of possibilities. What you and I should do now is abandon this booth, dance some more, share a plate of supper, perhaps chat to a few people and leave reluctantly."

In other words, they weren't going home straight away even though nothing else illegal was likely to be happening. Lucy thought about this as she fox-trotted energetically, the fringes of her New York dress swinging against her legs. She finished the dance laughing and breathless, agreeing with Jack within the hearing of at least two waiters that supper and another glass of lager would be splendid and saying what a jolly club this was.

An hour later, as Jack hailed an empty taxi, she said in a low voice, "Smoke and mirrors, am I right?"

For answer, he chatted gaily and inconsequently all the way to Edgar Mansions. It was only when they were inside her flat that his levity fell away.

Lucy went into the kitchenette to make tea. "You were worried they'd find the packet missing and suspect you of taking it out of the cupboard. That's why we were making Bright Young Fools of ourselves."

He leaned against the door jamb, pensive and dangerous at the same time. "Yes. Deflecting suspicion. At the risk of sounding like an insufferable male animal, I could wish you hadn't been with me."

"If I hadn't been with you, you wouldn't have found it."

"Why do you invariably have a good answer? We'll have to go back tomorrow evening and make sure to stay in the middle of the room, fully visible and well away from any booths."

"Perhaps you should have left the packet there," she said, turning off the gas ring and pouring boiling water into the teapot.

Jack got the cups and saucers down from the shelf. "Do you know, I can hear Uncle Bob saying exactly the same thing."

"Where did you stay last night?"

"With Lucy," said Jack evenly. The package lay on the table between them. His uncle hadn't quite said he should have left well alone, but the words hovered in the air.

"Was that wise?"

"I thought so, yes. If, and it's a big if, the drugs were for onward distribution, not Kent caching his personal supply in case he was searched, they wouldn't discover it was missing until after we had left. Maybe not at all. There would be no reason for anyone to follow us at that point unless it was out of curiosity because they knew me. If they *did* discover the packet had vanished and they remembered I was in that booth, they had my address. Both circumstances made staying at Lucy's flat seem a good idea. She might not like the thought of me protecting her, but that's never going to stop me doing it."

Curtis awarded him a long look. "You'd better marry that young woman sharpish."

"I would if you'd stop dispatching me across the channel on undercover missions."

Curtis ignored this. "I'll send this for analysis, but on the face of it, it looks like the same packaging as the heroin you recovered on the Atlantic Princess. It would be very satisfactory to trace them back to a common distribution agent."

"You mentioned George Forrest putting up the money for the Black Cat club," murmured Jack.

"And his longtime associate Edward Carter was enjoying the millionaire life on board the Atlantic Princess. I know. The principle they drum into us in the police is not to jump to conclusions."

"Tedious for you," said Jack.

"The first task is a discreet sweep of the place. I'll take Miss Lucy's advice and put in one of our cleaners." He made a note. "I'll also run a check on Mr Paul Kent. He could be a user."

"I did investigate the firm briefly for anything that could be useful to Lucy."

"What did you find?" asked his uncle.

"The practice has been established for over sixty years and appears to be on the level. Kent Senior has retired. Kent and his sister are both directors. Kent has been married to the American heiress Marion Bell for some fifteen years. She was the Toast of the Season when her family came over looking for a title. Several eminent gentlemen were in the running, but Kent swept all before him. Their first child was born suspiciously early, which may have been a factor in his victory. I'll have another browse through the newspaper archives in case there was something I missed."

Curtis grunted. "The heroin packet could also have been left there by any of the employees of the Black Cat club. The idiots who queered your pitch yesterday can call back asking for a staff list. Make out it's routine. It shouldn't be beyond their capability."

Jack pricked up his ears at the caustic tone. "Weren't they supposed to be there, then?"

"They were not. They fancied having a drink on duty and exercising a bit of power. They've had some advice about that from their divisional super who could have used their presence at a brothel he was taking apart above a gentlemen's club four streets away. Forget them. Who else might know how to open the concealed cupboard? Anyone who owns one or who has seen it demonstrated, presumably. Any chance of finding out how widespread they are?"

Jack said with some reluctance, "Lucy is going to mention the similarity in design casually in the office today and watch for a reaction."

His uncle looked at him, his face unreadable. "And you are both going back to the Black Cat again tonight."

"We are. Just another idle, well-heeled couple looking for amusement and distraction. Besides, I found this in the paper yesterday."

Curtis read through the advert. "Happy and comfortable, eh? H&C. Heroin and cocaine. You didn't show me this before you went there."

"I didn't spot it until after I'd left you. Yesterday was Friday. The advert - if it is referring to the Black Cat club - says Saturday."

"You have remembered that after your last brush with drug smugglers, you and Lucy are supposed to be staying well away from any operation with a whiff of dope to it."

"I know, but it would look more suspicious if we didn't make at least one return visit. I will look after her and we will not be sitting in any booths. Oh, I nearly forgot. What do you know about Consolidated Cocoa? Chap by the name of Trelawny."

A look of mild interest came over Curtis's face. "Nothing. Should I?"

"According to a typist in Lucy's office, they are paying out twelve shillings a quarter on a ten pound unit share and have been steadily for some years."

His uncle whistled. "That's a hell of a return, even for the commodities market. Going to follow it up?"

"I certainly am. My journalistic instincts are telling me there's a story. Can you save me some time by finding out where the registered office is?"

Curtis spoke briefly into the telephone, then scribbled an address and pushed it across the table. "There you are. Let me know how you get on."

Jack got up, collecting his hat and gloves from the side table. "Always do."

London streets amused Lucy. There were far fewer horse-drawn carts and vans than there were in Newmarket, and many more motor cars and buses, but the people themselves were just as busy, just as full of their own concerns. Ladies' hats were more fashionable, of course. There were more silk headscarves to be seen than serviceable wool. Gentlemen, though, were alike everywhere. Suited, overcoats in sober colours, hats worn at a range of angles, and every one of them carrying an umbrella against the mere possibility of rain.

Watching people was Lucy's consolation for not spending the day writing. Going to work on Saturday, even if only for the morning, was a distinct effort after dancing the evening away at the Black Cat club. If it wasn't for her hidden agenda, she would have put the bare minimum effort into her typing. As it was, she had to be wide awake when it was time for Miss Kent to come downstairs with the weekly pay packets. Lucy hung up her coat, took off her hat and gloves, and settled down with one eye on the clock.

She wasn't the only one. Miss Hodge was still talking about yesterday's treat. "They were lovely buns. Smithy will be sorry to have missed them. Did I tell you I'm going down to Hampshire to her folks to visit her this weekend? Gosh, I do miss her. It's not the same, rattling about in our little flat by myself. I hope there isn't too much work today. If I leave dead on one o'clock and hurry, I can catch the early train from Waterloo."

"Give her our good wishes," said Miss Reed.

"Yes, do," said Mrs Corrigan, "and please thank her mother again for the drop scone recipe using sour milk. I've blessed it this summer. Milk goes off so quickly in sultry weather, even on the cold shelf."

The room soon echoed to the sound of typewriters, with frequent exclamations of annoyance when keys jammed or a mistake necessitated the redoing of a page. Lucy had put considerable thought into how to introduce the subject of the Black Cat club without it being obvious that she was fishing for information. Accordingly, just before Miss Kent was due downstairs, she nipped out of the office and loitered in the hallway studying the framed plans.

"Are you looking for something in particular, Miss Brown?"

Lucy gave a convincing start. "Oh, Miss Kent. I was just on my way back from the..." She indicated the conveniences at the end of the passage. "Then I remembered I was going to look and see if there was a design for a nightclub here."

Miss Kent looked coolly amused. "I don't believe so. Why?"

"My fiancé took me to the Black Cat club yesterday evening and the bench seats in the booths were just like yours."

"A coincidence, I imagine. What was this club like?"

"Very modern. The main room was down in a basement and had slim box pillars with clever lighting to make it look vaulted, but I don't think it could have been. Not in Soho. The colour scheme was lovely, all gold and cinnamon and turquoise. We really went for the floor show. My fiancé had heard it was very good."

There was no amusement on the older woman's face now. Rather, she had an air of inner calculation. "And was it?"

"Goodness, yes. Anyway, I just wondered, because of the bench seats. Yours are so stylish. That's why I noticed them."

"Thank you. Mr Koivisto designed them. He is something of an artist when it comes to working in wood. His furniture always sells well. You could have simply asked Miss Reed about the designs. She is as knowledgeable as anyone in the company."

I could if I'd thought. Lucy paused with her hand on the doorknob, visited by sudden inspiration. "Oh, it would have been too insensitive with Mrs Corrigan worried because her landlord has put their rent up by two bob a week. Saying we'd been spending so frivolously when she's having to make drop scones with sour milk rather than letting it go to waste would rub it in horribly, wouldn't it?"

"I suppose it would. Your feelings do you credit, Miss Brown."

A few moments later, Miss Kent followed her through the door, her usual brisk self. She gave Miss Reed her wages first as protocol demanded, then handed Miss Hodge her envelope. "You are looking very smart. Are you going out for lunch?"

"I'm visiting Miss Smith this weekend. Her mother has invited me to stay. It will be lovely to see her, even if she is still poorly."

"Give her our best wishes for her recovery." Miss Kent smiled. "You must miss her. You share rooms, do you not? I daresay the work of the company will not suffer if you leave half an hour early to make sure you catch the train."

Miss Hodge beamed. "Thank you, Miss Kent."

Lucy received her envelope next, then Miss Kent stopped at the corner table. "Mrs Corrigan, I'm sure your children are looking forward to spending the afternoon with you, but I have a report that has to be typed today so I can study the figures over the weekend. I wonder if you might be very kind and stay for an extra hour? You can send the messenger boy with a note so your husband won't worry."

Mrs Corrigan flushed with gratitude. "I'd be happy to, Miss Kent."

"Thank you. I will bring it down later."

Lucy silently congratulated herself. That would be another sixpence towards the rent and with any luck, more occasional work would be put Mrs Corrigan's way.

CHAPTER FIVE

Christina Kent went upstairs thoughtfully. She distributed the wage envelopes to the draughtsmen and was unsurprised when, two minutes after she had entered her own room, she heard the door open and close behind her.

"Tired, Christina?"

She came out of her reverie and gave Vilho a faint smile. "No, or no more so than usual. I'm puzzled. Possibly worried."

"Anything I can help with?"

"Maybe. The new typist - who is no fool, by the way - has just asked if we have ever designed nightclubs, because her fiancé took her to one last evening where there were booths with the same bench seats as mine."

Vilho shrugged ruefully. "I am evidently not as unique in my ideas as I thought. I agree with you about Miss Brown. I had an interesting conversation with her about utility space in small apartments which will be useful for the Carter Industries housing."

Even through her worry, Christina couldn't help smiling. Vilho was always thinking about designs, always using every scrap of knowledge that came his way. She continued. "Miss Brown also described slim faux-pillars in this club with clever lighting to make the basement room look airy and modern, yet cosy and exciting."

Vilho's attention sharpened. His grey-blue eyes that had always seemed to Christina to reflect the lakes of his native Finland, held hers. "Pillars? What colour was this clever lighting?"

"Gold, cinnamon and turquoise. She has quite a way with words, does Miss Brown."

"Someone," said Vilho evenly, "is stealing our designs."

They contemplated each other. "It's not the first time," replied Christina at last.

"No. This feels like fragments of our work being copied and put together to make a different jigsaw. Did you get the name of the club? We could do a show this evening and then go on to this place for supper."

"The Black Cat, somewhere in Soho. I can't, Vilho, I told Papa I would visit this weekend." Not that he wanted her for herself, it was Paul he was interested in hearing news of, it always had been.

"Then I will go alone. And before you drive to Radlett, I will accompany you on your midday walk, steer you into the Copper Grill and make sure you eat lunch. You are too apt to lose yourself in thought and then tell your woman you have eaten when you have done no such thing. Not liking to be fussed is no excuse for starvation."

She smiled and touched his face fleetingly. "You know me very well."

"And have loved you even longer. But I can wait."

"I am sorry, Vilho, but I promised my mother..."

"That you would look after Garth and Paul. I do not think it was fair of Diana to ask you as she lay dying, but I respect it. I would point out, as I have done many times before, that you could look out for them just as well if we were married."

Dearest Vilho. How could she ever tell him that if she were married to him, he would take precedence in all her thoughts and actions? That promises made to her mother would be as dust. That her father and her brother could destroy themselves in a hundred different ways and she would never notice. "Come with me," she said impulsively. "I'm not taking Nanny so there will be room in the car. Papa would like that. He always asks after you."

"No."

"Why not?"

Vilho smiled with great tenderness. "Because I too made a promise to your mother."

No time like the present, thought Jack after dropping into *The Times* office for a dip into the society archives of 1912 and to file a highly moral piece on the licentious behaviour of several outwardly respectable gentlemen who had been arrested whilst taking advantage of a party of wretched, misguided females. His editor would no doubt tone it down, but enough emphasis that the police were increasing their vigilance on dubious places of pleasure should survive to give anyone thinking of coercing unwilling women pause for thought.

Seductively high returns on investments sounded like another article that would earn him a crust while he investigated bigger and more nebulous stories. On the way to South Belgravia where Consolidated Cocoa was based, he ran through various methods of approach. Arriving, these narrowed down to one. It was a large house, now sublet to a number of different businesses. With his hat at a jaunty angle and swinging his umbrella in a carefree manner, Jack hurried up the steps as if he had every right to be there.

Consolidated Cocoa, it seemed from the printed card next to one of the bell pushes, was on the second floor. He opened the front door, holding it politely for two earnest-faced young men deep in conversation. A messenger boy rushed in, calling a cheeky "Ta, guv," before disappearing into the nether reaches of the ground floor. From various doors came the sound of muted conversation and the clack of typewriters. Jack nodded with satisfaction and ran lightly up the stairs to the second floor, adopting the persona of a cheerful clerk who'd started work in one of the other offices and was hunting for like-minded companions for a chat over a cigarette. He left his umbrella in a corner at the top of the stairs and knocked on the Consolidated Cocoa door.

There was no answer. He knocked again. Still no answer.

Jack had many skills not acquired through the medium of formal education. The one he employed now had been imparted to him by a gentleman called Fingers when they were trapped in a foxhole in France a decade ago. Keeping a sharp watch up and down the corridor while he manipulated the lock, he presently slipped inside the door.

The office was a decent size, functional, but devoid of personality. In the centre of the room stood a standard desk and chair with a covered typewriter. A four-drawer index-card cabinet was on a side table next to it. Two hard chairs and a coat stand occupied the corner. A further table against the wall held a tray of crockery and a careless fan of post. Jack was interested to see the post included an envelope in his own handwriting. Evidently one of yesterday's adverts referring to 'small stakes, steady returns' led to Consolidated Cocoa. Mr Trelawny must have collected his mail from the post office box this morning and left it on the table to go through later.

A quick survey of the window at the back of the room disclosed a narrow sill along which it was just possible a desperate person could reach the fire escape. Jack noted it for emergencies then, expecting the return of Trelawny at any moment, went swiftly through the contents of the desk.

The top drawer contained a stack of empty envelopes with typed addresses and a sheaf of cheques for various multiples of twelve shillings made out to Consolidated Cocoa investors. A cursory comparison showed the names on the envelopes matched those on the cheques. Only the first few had been signed. A locked lower drawer contained a large notebook with names, dates and stakes. On the other side of the desk, drawers held fresh envelopes, a supply of postage stamps, three part-used cheque books and a spare. On the index cards were written names in alphabetical order, together with addresses, initial number of units purchased and subsequent ones added underneath. What there *wasn't* was anything to do with cocoa. No records, no financial ledgers, no tables of forecasts.

With the tingle in his blood that always told him he was on to a story, Jack made a note of Consolidated Cocoa's bank branch and account number, replaced everything as he had found it and exited, considering his next move. That there was a fiddle in place, he was in no doubt. That it targeted those members of society least able to afford it was also clear, given the humble nature of the majority of unit-holders' addresses. The story needed breaking and splashing all over the papers.

A number of doors on this floor sported blank name holders. He recollected several of the bell pushes had been similarly unlabelled. If ever there was an occasion to nip along to the letting agents and enquire about taking an office for himself, this was it. Consolidated Cocoa would bear keeping under observation.

It was soon done. The transaction completed, Jack stowed the keys in his pocket and proceeded to his next port of call.

Part of his usefulness to his uncle was his ability to move in circles where the presence of the police had a discouraging effect on conversation. One such circle included the apparently conservative banker George Forrest who was financing the Black Cat club.

It was Forrest's custom after finishing work on a Saturday to lunch at the Portland Club then play bridge for a couple of hours before departing for a weekend of domestic felicity in the leafy suburb of Hampstead. This programme had his wife's full approval. Mrs Forrest bore her obligatory appearances as his spouse with forbearance, but was happiest when left to herself, her household and her children.

Unlike the Bath Club, the Portland was not for the frivolously-minded. Jack had established himself years ago as a serious, occasionally brilliant card player, and had no difficulty today making up a four with Forrest and a couple of others. At first they played in silence, but after the first couple of hands, desultory conversation was generally the order of the day.

"Pardon me," said Jack, stifling a yawn. "Dropped in at the Black Cat club last night after taking my fiancée to a show and we stayed later than intended."

He didn't miss the swift look Forrest gave him, but it was the gentleman currently twiddling his thumbs as dummy who said, "The Black Cat? Isn't that one of your investments, Forrest?"

"Not for much longer," said the banker. "I backed it originally but there has been a difference of opinion with the owners. What did you think of it, Sinclair?"

"Frightfully amusing. The band was well known and played all the latest numbers. Top notch set of dancers. Funny how some places have that certain something to them and some don't."

His partner looked interested. "And this place does? Maybe you've been too hasty in getting rid of it, Forrest."

"You can tell it's been thought about," continued Jack. "Decent sprung floor for dancing and a good, stylish decor. It hasn't been thrown together like a lot of these clubs, with dim lighting and a splash of gilt. It's funny how spending money on a place makes you want to stay longer. I don't think we sat down for more than half an hour last night, and that was mostly to eat supper."

"What it is to be young," said Jack's partner, laying down the queen of diamonds, only to see it disappear under the five of hearts. "Damn you, Forrest, I thought I'd accounted for all the small trumps. Game to you."

And game to me too, thought Jack. He'd bet even Uncle Bob didn't know Forrest was selling his stake in the Black Cat club. He wondered very much what the 'differences of opinion' had been. And with who?

One o'clock at last. Lucy came out into the hall in her hat and coat and nearly walked into Aidan coming in through the front door. "Hello," she said, surprised and pleased. "That was quick. I only posted my letter to you yesterday morning. Miss Reed, this is my brother, Aidan. I've told you about him. He's training to be a doctor."

"Very nice to meet you. I will see you on Monday, Miss Brown."

Aidan cast a wild glance at Mr Kent's door.

Lucy saw him looking. "It's a good thing you didn't barge in there to find me," she said, pulling on her gloves. "That's Mr Kent's room. Gentlemen callers are supposed to wait outside, even if they are my brother. You've cut it fine. Another few minutes and you would have missed me. No one would be here at all, not even the receptionist."

"Sorry," said Aidan distractedly. "I was studying."

"Never mind, you're here now which is lovely. You rushed off so quickly the other day. I was hoping we might travel together and have a good natter on the train."

"I didn't know how long you were staying and I had to

get back." He glanced over his shoulder at the front door. "Fancy place."

Aidan was behaving very oddly, almost as if he was nervous. She tucked her arm in his. "It suits me for the moment. Come on, I'll buy lunch while you tell me what's eating you."

"Nothing," he said, with the unconvincing air that had never fooled her.

"Am I or am I not your older sister? For a start, why do you need money?"

His face was a picture. "How did you know?"

"Am I or am I not...?"

"All right, all right. I can't tell you, Lucy."

She looked at him, direct and honest. "Are you in trouble?"

"Not me. A friend."

Lucy's mind performed what she maintained was intuition but other people decried as leaping to conclusions. "The girl Mother mentioned?"

"How do you *do* that?" asked Aidan. "Yes. She's in a rotten contract and wants to buy out of it."

"Don't do anything illegal in order to help her."

"Why would you think I might?"

"Because you went off with Basil Milcombe," said Lucy bluntly.

"Oh, Basil. What does he understand about being in debt? Him with his prize money and stud fees and dividends and winning bets?"

"Here's a Lyons. Their daily special is usually good." Lucy waited until they were seated and had given their orders, then put her hand over her brother's. "Is there really nothing I can help with? How much do you need?"

"A gentleman doesn't borrow money off his sister," said Aidan stiffly.

"A sensible gentleman doesn't borrow off Basil Milcombe either."

"I haven't," said her brother, exasperated. "He saw I was short in the wind and he's paying me to do a couple of small jobs for him, that's all."

"Lawful jobs?"

"Yes! It's delivering things he is too busy to take care of himself and doesn't want to trust to the post."

"See it stays that way. Meanwhile, if your young lady needs a friend, you know where I live. At least, I assume you do, even though I haven't seen you there for months."

"You're starting to sound like Mother," warned Aidan with the glimmer of his usual smile.

Lucy smiled back. "What's her name?"

"Daisy," said her brother, as if the very word itself was made of spun gold.

Daisy. It would be. And she'll be helpless and fragile, with big blue eyes and a sob story. Oh Aidan. "Good sturdy name," said Lucy cheerfully. "Daisies grow in the most unpromising places. How did you meet her?"

"She was in front of me hurrying for a bus and she tripped. I helped her up but she'd sprained her ankle, so I got a bandage from the chemist and strapped it up. Then we sat on a bench and talked for a while and then I saw her back to her hostel. She doesn't mind that it'll take me a while to be qualified. I've never met anyone like her before. Imagine, she's never been out of London."

"In that case she'll either love the countryside or run screaming back to the railway station as soon as you take her to meet the family."

Whether it was her prosaic attitude or he really did have studying to do, Aidan didn't linger after the meal. Lucy, plunging into the underground as the quickest way home to spend an uninterrupted afternoon on her latest detective novel, considered that her brother had given her plenty of food for thought.

After the cheerful warmth of the Copper Grill, the car was cold and the sky ahead distinctly grey. Christina's capable hands rested on the steering wheel, waiting for a tangle of buses to sort themselves out ahead. Edgware Road to Elstree, then Watling Street to Radlett. How many times had she done this trip over the years?

Radlett had been her home right up until the moment when 'Garth Kent Architects' became 'Kent and Son, Architects' and she realised neither her father nor her brother considered her significant enough to be named in the company. The fact that she was a full partner, had been articled to her father for longer than Paul, and had taken over the day-to-day handling of the finances several years before didn't weigh with them at all.

Not that she'd shown how deep the knife thrust had been. She had simply stated her intention of taking Nanny and moving into the top floor of the Fitzroy Square building. She had pointed out that now Paul was married with a London house of his own and Marion to act as his hostess, he didn't need company accommodation after late-night client dinners. This would save her doing the journey twice a day and ensure someone was always here to keep an eye on the place.

Vilho had applauded her decision and had set about redesigning the flat to fit her personality. If he'd asked her then to marry him, she might have given in, but being a gentleman who had already received several perfectly friendly rebuffs, he hadn't. Thus they continued their easy working relationship based on mutual respect and appreciation of the other's qualities. Easy, familiar and comforting. She and Nanny had lived here ever since. From here she had kept the firm going during the war, with Miss Reed's faithful assistance, while Vilho was on transoceanic convoy duty, Paul saw out the hostilities in a defence garrison on the coast and her father drummed up whatever work he could find.

Radlett held bittersweet memories. It had been too many years to count, yet she knew walking into the drawing room would again evoke the powerful emotion of seeing Vilho for the first time. The room lit by the setting sun and Paul, home from university that first vacation, saying carelessly, "I've brought Koivisto with me, that's all right, isn't it? I've told you about him. Wizard with a set square."

Christina had looked up, a conventional smile of welcome on her lips, and had felt her heart turn over. She heard the rustle of her mother's gown as she stood to give her hand to the stranger, heard the note of indulgence in her father's voice as he said any friend of Paul's was welcome in the Kent household and had been struck entirely dumb.

At twenty, Vilho Koivisto had been slim, of romantic appearance, with fair hair worn student-style and with eyes that seemed to see right into her soul. And then he smiled and said something she had no recollection of now and held out his hand for her to shake and she took it and knew she was in love.

Vilho walked back from the garage where Christina kept her car, considering how best to utilise his afternoon. The proposal for Fraser and Timmins on Monday was finished. Enhancing it now would be counter-productive. He would have liked to spend the hours talking over ideas with Christina for the new apartments that a surprisingly enlightened factory owner wanted built to house his workforce. Two double blocks, back to back, separated by gardens for promenading and exercise. Each flat compact but well constructed, with natural light and modern conveniences so the workers would stay rather than chasing better paid jobs elsewhere. He would get on with the floor plans anyway. Then on Monday, Christina would replace them with something more practical and they would be away.

The beginning of a project was always an adventure. Paul was enthused enough to see the initial potential and engage with the client. That was his forté. He would no doubt look at the plans half-way through and add embellishments, but it was Vilho and Christina who made a proposal work.

Paul was a hedonist in work as well as in life. All the glory, none of the graft. Flashes of brilliance, but fewer by far than there used to be. He had grown lazy, coasting instead of putting in the hard work. He could charm the birds off the trees, could Paul, and was persistent in pursuit of a contract, but it was many years now since Vilho had seen through the glamour.

"And yet I still work for him," said Vilho aloud. He smiled ruefully. The reason, as it had been from the first moment he saw her, the first moment he felt the touch of her palm against his, was Christina.

CHAPTER SIX

In the lobby of Edgar Mansions, Lucy nodded in a friendly fashion to the concierge, unlocked her mailbox, sped down to the end of the row and silently checked the box for Phoebe Sugar's room, then turned the keys in both lockers and took the lift to the third floor. Phoebe had a useful cheque to pay in on Monday. She also had a memo from the *Chronicle* suggesting a number of places at which she might photograph the latest darlings of the social pages.

"Suggestions," said Lucy aloud with a snort. What they meant was that the paper had been given a consideration to cover them. She ran her eye down the list and laughed aloud. Well now, that was useful. But also tricky. First, however, she had a book to write.

Two hours later, she heard the sound of Jack's key in the door. "Can you type anywhere?" he asked, coming into the lounge looking preoccupied.

Lucy took a moment to free herself from the scene. "I can type anywhere, yes. If you are asking whether I can write anywhere, only if no one is talking to me."

"Jolly good. Bring the typewriter. I'll nab a taxi."

Lucy resigned herself to getting no work done for the remainder of the afternoon. "Where are we going?"

"Consolidated Cocoa. There was no one there this morning, but it looked as though they'd be in later. I have taken the adjoining office. We can either get to know them, or you can sit at the desk typing while I have a snoop."

She had to hand it to him. Being with Jack was never boring. "You only want me for my ability to stand on a chair screeching about a mouse if somebody comes along the corridor."

"That's the idea. Do you mind?"

"Not at all." It was true. For the sake of Miss Reed's investments, she was as keen to know what was going on as Jack was. And it was *nice* working on things together.

In the taxi, she told him about her brother. "So that's why he wants money, to release Daisy from her contract."

Jack frowned. "Aidan didn't ask for money, and he didn't want to tell you any more about this girl. Then why go to the trouble of meeting you from the office?"

Lucy shrugged. "Guilt after getting my letter? Also, judging by the speed at which his steak special disappeared, he was hungry. His scruples don't extend to not lunching at my expense."

At Lower Belgrave Street, Jack led her up two floors, gave her a neatly typed card to slot in the holder on the door, then felt in his pocket for the key.

"Elljay Associates," she read as she inserted the card. "How touching. What line of business are we in?"

"No idea. You can decide. Anything except private detectives."

"Accountants? Then no one will think anything of you sitting here copying lists into ledgers. It's what they seem to do all day long."

Jack grinned. "You haven't ever fancied researching *Angela Andrews: Accountant* for one of your career girl adventures, then?"

She looked at him severely. "I have not. Even for those books, I have to be able to identify at least a little bit with the passion the poor heroines feel for their job. I can't do that with columns of figures. It's a shame, though, because there are all sorts of good titles I could use if I set a detective novel in a financial firm. *Adding Up To Murder* maybe, or *The Bottom Line Is Death.*"

"Never say never. Write them down and save them for when we need to find school fees for six children and no one is commissioning socialites' photographs or journalistic investigations any more."

He opened the door on to a plain office with two functional tables, three upright chairs and a filing cabinet that had seen better days.

Children. A casual assumption that they'd be starting a family, that they would be together forever. Lucy put the typewriter rather abruptly on the table facing the door, hung her coat and hat on the stand, then busied herself arranging a stack of paper. She found her heart was beating abnormally fast and her legs were not quite steady.

"We'd better buy some principles-of-accountancy books from the second hand stalls and scatter them on the shelves," she said. "Maybe a dispirited pot plant."

"Can't we buy a nice one?"

"It wouldn't last. Gardening is something else I have yet to master."

"Another career to research. *Death Amongst the Delphiniums. The Apple Orchard Murders.* Marriage to you is going to be enormous fun, Lucy." His dancing eyes met hers, his inner excitement arrowing out of him and straight into her heart.

Her smile grew. Life with Jack would always be an adventure. "It will," she agreed. "Go on, next door with you and have a snoop."

She heard him knock, heard the click of a lock. The rest of the floor was quiet.

"Can you type these names and addresses?" he asked, returning with a large notebook.

She grinned. "I can do better than that." She got her trusty pocket Kodak out of her working satchel. "We don't want to be here all night, do we?"

Every time Jack thought he had the measure of Lucy, she surprised him. Leaving her to take photographs of Trelawny's list of clients, he returned next door. He looked longingly at the scatter of letters that hadn't been moved since this morning. No, it wasn't safe to even try. He scanned the room again.

"There's no phone next door," he said, going back to where Lucy was looking adorably professional. "That's odd for a commodities broker, wouldn't you say?"

"Very odd. Everything office-based needs a phone. How does he manage? Uses the box on the corner? Sorry, Jack, you're going to have to hold these pages open for me."

"Right you are." He spread the pages while she took photographs.

"There, finished. Any more?"

"Several hundred index cards that I daren't disarrange. Nothing else in the desk of any significance. There ought to be though. There ought to be a bank book, or at the very least a proper financial ledger."

"Maybe Trelawny keeps those at home."

"How inconvenient of him. You have a look while I keep watch. Tell me what I've missed."

Lucy obligingly followed him next door and glanced around. "I don't think much of the cleaner. There's a film of dust on everything." She peered underneath the typewriter cover. "This has been used recently." Her gaze travelled on to the tray of crockery. "Those haven't. Where does he make tea? There's no tap or gas ring in here."

"Kitchenette at the far end of the corridor, next to the lavatory."

"It's a lot of crockery just for one person, right at the edge of the table too. If you caught it accidentally it would be on the floor."

"That might be deliberate to deter sneak thieves."

But Lucy was frowning at the floor now. It was standard parquet flooring like the office next door, but where the side table was, there were faint marks as if the table had once been further out towards the centre. "There are scrapes on the floor."

Jack left his post at the doorway and squatted down to look. He stood up again, eyeing the table. "I wonder... move the tray of crockery on to the desk. Then keep watch in the corridor."

Lucy did so. "You think there's a loose floorboard? I've used that idea before."

"Simpler than that," he said. Following the scrape marks, he carefully pulled the table away from the wall to reveal the front of a desk. "It's a second desk. The drawers were hidden against the wall." He gently manipulated the lock on the nearest drawer. "And lo..."

"What have you found?"

"A bank book. We need to take photographs of the pages quick and then lock up."

Lucy dashed back into their own office and got the camera. Jack spread the pages while she snapped.

"Now we put everything back," he said, relocking the drawer and pushing the desk to its previous position. "I don't want to risk Trelawny coming in with the afternoon post and finding us in situ. In fact, I want to get out of here completely, just in case. Are you all right leaving your typewriter until tomorrow?"

"If you like. Something tells me I'm not going to get any more writing done today. Where are we off to now if it isn't straight home again?"

"I thought we might invite ourselves to tea with Jimmy and Gina Ward, assuming they are in town."

"They are. Gina finished making her final film, then Jimmy took her to Paris for a few days for a delayed honeymoon. She sent me a postcard saying they were flying back yesterday. Flying! I think that's why she wrote. She was dying to tell someone."

"She can describe it all in person then. I want a word with Jimmy about the likelihood of making a twenty-four percent return on cocoa."

"Twenty-four percent?" Jimmy Ward stared at his friend meditatively. "No, I don't see it. Who did you say this cove was?"

"Name of Trelawny. Consolidated Cocoa."

Jimmy shook his head slowly. Behind the blank facade, Jack knew he was reviewing every commodities firm in the City of London. "No, don't know them."

Which was what Jack had suspected. "Then how is he paying twelve shillings a quarter on a ten pound unit stake?"

"Oh, that's easy. Working capital."

"I beg your pardon?"

"Working capital. Say this chap is a mechanic. Wants his own garage, but can't raise the wind. He knows no one will invest in an untried outfit, so he invents a sure-fire returns bond and persuades susceptible blighters to entrust him with their hard-earned cash which he uses to set himself up. Pays them back in dribs and drabs out of his income so he doesn't get investigated. Four years later, the company quietly disappears."

Jack looked at him with respect. "It's a good thing you've never taken to crime, Jimmy. You'd be terrifying."

His friend blinked, genuinely bemused. "Who needs

crime when you've got business. That's exciting enough for me."

"Poor Miss Reed," said Lucy. "I wonder how I can suggest she asks for her units back."

"You can't," said Gina. "People hate thinking they've been made fools of. Have you really been working in an office? Haven't you been having fun at all?"

"We went to the Black Cat last night. Really good floor show, but my goodness the dancers' costumes didn't leave much to the imagination."

Gina gave a professional nod. "I know what you mean. A length of silk and don't care. I'm glad I've left those days behind. Have you had enough tea? Come and see the lovely clothes Jimmy bought me in Paris."

Jack grinned at his friend as the girls disappeared. "Marriage suiting you, then?"

"I don't want it ever to stop. I'm the luckiest man alive. When are you two tying the knot?"

Jack helped himself to another piece of cake with an ease he was far from feeling. "Need to wait for Charles to get back from foreign parts so he can be best man. He'll never forgive me otherwise."

"You won't regret it."

No, but Lucy might. He remembered the time he'd been set on in the docks at Marseilles, that hit-and-run in New York... He needed to disentangle himself from his various undercover work before he had any right to name a date.

"Do you want to do a show before we go to the Black Cat club tonight?" he asked once they were back at Lucy's flat.

"Ah," she said. "I was going to mention that."

"We don't have to go if you don't want to, but we need to do something equally visible in case anyone is suspicious about the missing packet of dope. Uncle Bob reminded me we are supposed to be steering clear of places with possible drug connections. These people have long memories."

Lucy raised her eyebrows. "In that case, we'd never go anywhere. And you can't say I'm wrong, because my knowledge comes directly from your newspaper articles."

He smiled wryly. "Touché. I did explain to him it would be more suspicious if we *didn't* go at least one more time."

A trace of guilt crossed Lucy's face. "That's good, because I don't think we have a choice. There was a note from the *Chronicle* when I got home today. They want Phoebe to contribute a couple of paragraphs with supporting photos on all the latest rich, glamorous people to grace the Black Cat club with their presence. I'm assuming the name of the *Chronicle* will act as a magic password and let me into the foyer, if not down to the dance floor. I'm sorry, Jack, I know we talked about retiring Phoebe, but she's jolly useful on the financial front."

"And we'll need the money once I'm no longer being a carefree playboy for Uncle Bob. All the same, I'm not bowled over by this particular notion. Youssif Arama is far from stupid. If he thinks you are there as two people, he's going to trust the pair of us as much as a mouse trusts a philanthropic cat."

"People see what they expect to see. He will have been in touch with the *Chronicle*, so he'll know they'll send someone. Hopefully the jazzy lighting will make it more difficult for him to recognise Phoebe as me. I have to take the assignment, Jack. Aside from it amounting pretty much to an order, it will get Phoebe back in the *Chronicle*'s good graces. They haven't forgiven her yet for Mrs Lester deciding not to give them an exclusive on the twins' double wedding."

Jack sighed, accepting the inevitable. After all, he wouldn't have thought twice if it had been his own skin at risk, not Lucy's. "Talking of the Lesters, it would be just our luck if they were there tonight as well. Theo said they were aiming to give the Black Cat club a go some time soon."

Lucy made a face. "Let's hope they are as unobservant as your friend Tufty. Julie and Amanda got to know me quite well as Phoebe at the Bay Sands Hotel."

"That was six weeks ago. The only thing that stays in their heads longer than a fortnight are the latest dance steps. And we always knew they'd have to meet you as Lucy eventually."

"The other thing that worries me is having to hang around as Phoebe waiting for people to arrive. It's going to take some speedy footwork to be her as well as me in the same place on the same night."

"How do you usually manage?"

"Usually I don't have to be me shortly afterwards. I splash out on a cab and come back here."

Jack paced the living room, considering the problem. "That could work. I know a cabbie who wouldn't mind lurking down a side street. I did a favour for him once so he won't talk. Stay there, I'll nip out and see if he's in the locality. What time do you want to get there?"

Lucy laughed. "I might have guessed you'd know someone. Nine-thirty or so?"

"All fixed," he said fifteen minutes later. "He's going to pick us up and drive us to the Black Cat club. You can then go in and do your stuff as Phoebe while I lurk in the cab having a game of cards with him, after which he will drive us both back here for you to change, and then turn around and drop us off at the end of Frith Street."

"Doesn't he mind losing an hour's fares?"

"He won't be losing a penny," said Jack drily. "I'm paying him."

"I'm glad to see you, Miss Christina, and that's a fact," said the housekeeper, bustling into the hall from the back quarters to welcome her.

"Good afternoon, Mrs Drake." Christina glanced towards the drawing room door. "Is it a bad day?"

"Not yet, but we've got the Smarts and the Paynes here for dinner as well as the doctor and the vicar, and you know the general always rubs Mr Kent up the wrong way. I said to Geddings, thank goodness for small mercies. Miss Christina can always be depended on for a bit of soothing syrup, not like Mr Paul. Asking for a loan for some pet project - not that I was listening - and then cutting back to London and not even staying the night when Mr Kent turned him down. And that the very day I got a letter from my daughter saying she's in a bad way with her latest and me worrying what I can do to help her."

What sort of project? Nothing he had discussed with her. Annoyance swept through her. "I'm sorry to hear about Betty. I hope she picks up again soon. At least being married to a doctor means she won't have medical fees to pay. As for my brother, I daresay he was busy. We've a lot of work on. When was this?"

Mrs Drake sniffed. "Last weekend. I'll say no more, but some people should appreciate what they've got and not hanker after what they don't need. You'll find your father in the drawing room. Kettle's on and I'll get the girl to carry your bag up to your room."

Christina drew a deep breath as Mrs Drake bustled away. Quite how her father could bear the housekeeper's incessant chatter she didn't know. The woman wasn't even a particularly good manager. He was used to her and he didn't like change, that was it. She opened the door and went in.

Garth Kent had been a big man with a big personality and a keen brain. He was still a big man, but whatever was eating away at his insides had caused him to fold in on himself. It hurt Christina to see it.

"Papa," she said, stooping to offer her cheek for his kiss. "You're looking well. Well enough for company tonight, I hear."

"I owed them a dinner and it's easier when you're here. Someone to do the pretty. How's business? The latest accounts look good."

"They are good. We have plenty of work. We've a meeting with Fraser and Timmins on Monday. I brought the proposal down for you to look through if you are interested." She laid the result of Mrs Corrigan's typing on the side table next to him.

Garth picked up the report, drummed his fingers on it, put it down again. "Paul's sound," he said. "He'll keep the firm going."

Christina drew off her gloves and sat down, thinking of expensive lunches and wasted afternoons on profitless clients. "He's much better than mixing with clients than I am, that's for sure. Did he mention the potential project for two double-blocks of workers' apartments for Carter Industries? I had no idea he even knew Edward Carter. He said one of his contacts recommended us. It would be a feather in our cap if we got it."

A trace of enthusiasm flickered over Garth's face. "New apartment blocks? It would give Vilho something useful to do rather than designing those modular houses he's so keen on. I said to Paul they'll never sell here. America, maybe. Not in this country. I told him if he can find a British builder willing to invest in the things - which he won't - then I'll consider releasing capital for the project. Not before. Paul should have known better than to suggest it. Not like him at all."

Christina's thoughts raced. That was so typical of her brother. Getting in first with Vilho's idea, even though he had been dismissive about it when Vilho spread his plans out. Neither Paul nor Garth, in her opinion, had the vision to see beyond the conventional. "When was this?" she asked. "Did he show you the drawings? They're very clever."

"Last weekend. Didn't show me the plans, just asked for capital to build some prototypes. Waste of money, which is what I told him. I should know. I've been in this business a darn sight longer than he has."

He was getting agitated. Christina moved his barley water within reach and said peaceably, "Vilho is very patient. It amuses him to design futuristic concepts. I don't think he is expecting anyone to build and market them just yet."

"Then why was Paul making such a fuss, eh?"

She would like to know that too. She watched as Garth picked up the Fraser and Timmins proposal again and subsided into a grumbling monologue about the cost of materials and labour. Just what was her brother up to?

CHAPTER SEVEN

Unlike Paul, Vilho did understand Miss Reed's filing system and he had a profound respect for her meticulous record keeping. In his silent office, he contemplated the blueprints spread out on the table and thought about the Kent family as he had first come to know them and as they were now. At twenty, he had been dazzled and grateful. A foreigner in an alien land, he had been welcomed with careless generosity. With maturity, he saw them rather more clearly.

Diana Kent had always been the peacemaker. Christina had inherited the role. Not, considered Vilho, altogether willingly. But with Garth and Paul ever ready to square up to each other, they had both taken their womenfolk's succour as an absolute right. They still did, all these years later. Christina continued to bolster her brother's character in front of Garth, looking after them both as she had promised. She knew Paul was still the favourite and agitation could prove fatal for a man in Garth's condition.

Vilho yearned to share that burden, to protect her, to be more than simply her steadfast friend and colleague. He looked at the blueprints again. He too had done his share of covering up for Paul, out of gratitude to Garth for taking him on, out of love for Christina. This latest transgression he was not sure could be hidden. The faux-pillar design had been his own, created for the Wentworth Gallery, and when Vilho had retrieved the plans from the archive he had found a note in Miss Reed's impeccable handwriting that not three months ago Paul Kent had logged them out and it had been a week before he returned them.

His thoughts circling uneasily in his head, Vilho put the plans back in their allotted space and locked up. He would change into evening dress, find somewhere to eat and then visit the Black Cat club to see for himself. Perhaps first-hand knowledge would help him decide what to do.

Dinner was over, the guests had gone. Garth Kent, testy with pain and nettled at his body's inability to keep going, had retired early with his medication, complaining fractiously to the doctor that the bottles didn't last as long as they used to and this latest prescription was no use anyway.

Christina was restless and troubled. When the ladies had withdrawn after the meal, Stella Payne had turned to her with a smile.

"My sister has thoroughly enjoyed their new conservatory this summer."

"They make a big difference," Christina had replied. "We have done a number of designs over the years."

"Yes, so your brother said, always tailored to the client's individual needs. Emily is delighted with it. He has such a clever touch."

Christina had kept her smile in place as Stella effused. Behind it, her thoughts were far from tranquil.

"Geddings," she said now, encountering the butler in the hall. "I'm going to bed. I don't think there is any point any of you waiting up. Tell me, Mrs Payne mentioned her sister over dinner and I cannot remember her married name. I didn't like to ask, she would have been so offended."

"Mrs James Durban."

"Of course. Thank you. Not that it matters in the least. I was simply annoyed with myself."

"Not surprising, miss, not with the amount you have to remember."

James and Emily Durban. Upstairs, Christina wrote down the names and stared at them. Cold stole over her, coating her heart with frost. She knew the practice had never submitted a design to them, never invoiced them, never received money from them. But someone evidently had, and Stella Payne seemed to think it had been Paul.

She looked around her bedroom. It was still as it had been when she'd moved to Fitzroy Square. Her brother's set of rooms, further down the passage, hadn't altered since his marriage. That was Garth, making believe nothing had changed when everything had, deceiving himself that he remained in charge of his empire.

Soft footed, hating herself for needing to be sure, Christina walked down to Paul's study, her green velvet gown moving fluidly around her ankles. Paul's old drawing board would still be set up, the chest of shallow drawers where he had kept his plans still in the corner of the room. Part of her didn't want to find anything. The new, frosted her was unsurprised when she pulled open the second drawer and saw a neatly detailed blueprint for 'Conservatory: Durban' laid on the surface. It was dated March of that year.

As she studied the plan, she felt anger flickering in her. Not content with taking on private work, Paul had copied this design from an earlier one the practice had drawn up for the Lucases of Westmoor Place. She rolled the drawer shut, then looked in the next one, and then the next. Throughout the chest she found evidence that Paul had been re-selling their designs to private clients. Her anger grew.

In the lowest drawer was his student portfolio. This at least would be all his own work. He had been young then, full of promising talent, king of the world. He had got a commendation from the School of Architecture for the 'striking originality' of his designs. When had he become so lazy? After his marriage to Marion with its attendant access to easy money? He had certainly pursued her hard enough for it. She opened the portfolio. A faint, elusive scent drifted up, reminding her of her mother.

Fifteen minutes later, Christina slipped through the door of the telephone cabinet in the hall. The phone in Vilho's flat rang out to emptiness. So too did the one in Fitzroy Square.

She replaced the receiver with a feeling of frustration. Upstairs, she paced around her room. The Black Cat club. That's where he'd said he'd be going. She wouldn't be able to contact him until the morning.

She looked out of her window at the gardens, still and silent in the moonlight. She thought about her car in the garage and had a sudden wild desire to throw off conventions, to be reckless for once in her life. She needed Vilho, she needed to talk to him, she needed to be in his presence. What would he think if she drove back now? What would he think if she walked into that club, if she appeared between the turquoise and cinnamon pillars and sat at his table? Would he understand? Would he accept her tacit offer? There would be no going back if he did. Christina thought of her best years slipping away like the miles of road under a set of powerful wheels. If not now, when? It wasn't that far back to London. She could do it in an hour at this time of night, maybe less. Did she dare?

Lucy swept past the commissionaire and into the Black Cat club, vivacious in pink and silver with an outrageous nodding feather headband encircling her blonde Marcel-waved wig.

"Phoebe Sugar. 'Society Snippets' in the *Chronicle*," she said, passing her card through the box office window and brandishing her camera. "I believe you are expecting me."

Youssif Arama stood immediately. "Certainly. It is gratifying that the *Chronicle* has sent you along with such... alacrity."

Hmm, not quite as pleased as he's pretending. "May I take photographs in here or would you rather I was outside?"

The manager waved a hand to indicate either. "But not downstairs," he said with a deprecating smile. "That is a members-only area."

Lucy inclined her head graciously and became very busy lining up shots. Tufty Thomas entered with a noisy party. Interestingly, one of the gentlemen on the periphery of the group hung back when the rest clattered downstairs and moved to the box office. Lucy frowned intently at her camera as if adjusting the lens. Out of the corner of her eye, she saw the gentleman beckoned up the short passage next to the booth, say a few words to Arama and then leave.

She made a mental note to mention it to Jack, then went outside and amused herself by taking a photograph of the doorman. "To get my eye in," she explained. "If you let me have your address, I'll send you a print."

The doorman, greatly pleased, stood to magnificent attention and vouchsafed the information that the programme at the Lyceum would finish in ten minutes and then there would be no end of smart folk along.

This proved to be the case. Lucy snapped a promising number of well-known society figures, including the Lester twins and their amiable viscounts.

"Phoebe!" squealed Amanda Lester. "Haven't seen you for simply ages. Sorry about the wedding. Mummy decided to book a studio to take the photographs. Wait until you hear about the reception, it's going to be such a laugh."

Lucy motioned them to all pose together in the doorway, the flashbulb went off and they disappeared laughing into the club. Another car drew up. It was certainly busy tonight. As Jack said, when word got around, it got around.

Eventually she had enough photographs to satisfy the *Chronicle* and the Black Cat club proprietors. She took one last shot of a film actress arriving, with her sleek businessman protector standing watchfully to one side. There were a couple of people in the background but that was all to the good. It made the shot look natural, not staged. The she nodded to the doorman and walked briskly away towards the side road where Jack was waiting.

"How did it go?" asked Jack once she was safely in the cab.

"Mr Arama put on a welcoming face, but he wasn't best pleased I had turned up quite this soon. He definitely relaxed when I took photos outside rather than in the lobby. I noticed a few non-nightclubby people. Solitary gentlemen who tagged on to other parties coming in but who didn't stay long. There must be offices behind the foyer. I happened to be facing that way when a man in a dinner suit emerged and Arama said loudly that it was perfectly all right to become a member. The gentleman looked startled, I thought."

Jack chuckled. "Well done. Here we are at home. Nip upstairs and turn into yourself. We want to get back there as soon as possible."

"Speak for yourself. I saw Basil Milcombe arriving just as I left. I'd rather not spend much time with him at all."

"We'll sit at the other side of the dance floor," promised Jack. "Go."

It wasn't long before Lucy was once more passing through the nightclub doorway, this time clinging to Jack's arm, dressed in her orange frock with flat dancing shoes on and a gauzy yellow scarf tied bandanna-style around her dark Egyptian bob.

As soon as they descended to the basement room, they were engulfed in noise from the band.

"I think tonight we join Tufty's party," murmured Jack. "At least to begin with."

Within moments they were part of the cheerful group, laughing fit to sprain their faces and putting up with sly jokes about not being *à deux* tonight. It was a relief to move to the dance floor for an energetic quick-step.

Coming back to the table, Lucy was astonished to see a familiar figure, dressed in an evening suit and standing irresolutely at the bottom of the stairs. She waved. "Aidan, over here!"

Her brother looked horrified, but crossed to the table.

"Twice in one day!" she said. "Don't tell me you are still delivering documents for Basil Milcombe?"

"No, there were only four and I've done them all."

"I didn't think you could be, especially as he's here himself."

"Is he?" Aidan looked incuriously where Lucy was pointing. Milcombe's party were seated at a table on the edge of the dance floor. All of them had the expansive look of soft livers and high spenders.

"Why are you here then? And how can you afford the entrance fee when only at lunchtime you were telling me you were saving every penny to..."

There was a clash of cymbals from the band. "And now, ladies and gentlemen, put your hands together for Rose Garden and the Kitten Kaboodle!"

Aidan's head whipped around towards the dance floor. One glance at her brother's rapt face told Lucy all she needed to know. His Daisy must be one of the Kittens. Following the direction of his gaze, she had a sinking feeling as to exactly which dancer she was.

The routine was as mesmerising as yesterday's offerings had been. As the dancers bowed and exited, delighted with their applause, Aidan let out a great sigh.

"Daisy," said Lucy.

Her brother nodded. "They're very good, aren't they? But she has to work so hard. They practise for hours every day. She doesn't mind that, she says she's used to it, but afterwards they have to socialise and... and sometimes worse. That's why I'm here."

The women were back, chivvied through the side door by the redhead. Rose, at a guess, though Lucy was as certain as it was possible to be that her birth certificate did not give Garden as a surname.

Basil had been in conversation with his noisy friends. "Rose," he called, and held up three fingers.

The leader of the troupe looked across, nodded and made to detach three of the girls. The pale, fair one went sheet white. Beside her, Aidan gave an indrawn hiss.

Praying that she was right in her guess, Lucy stood up. "Daisy," she shouted, waving and smiling. "You were great. Come and join us! Bring a friend."

The fair girl gasped, looked across and saw Aidan, grabbed the hand of the girl next to her and wove between the tables without looking back.

"Thank you," she whispered, as everyone boisterously shuffled chairs to make space for them. "Do I know you?"

Lucy pulled her into the sort of society embrace she saw so often when photographing the rich and famous for the *Chronicle*. "Lucy Brown. I'm Aidan's sister," she muttered. "Act as if you've known me for years." And rather louder, she said, "I mean it, that was extraordinary. How do none of you crash into each other?"

"Practice," said the second girl with a sigh. "Hours and hours of practice."

"Oh sorry," said Daisy, with more acumen than Lucy had expected. "Enid, this is Lucy Brown, Aidan's sister. Lucy, Enid Bursall."

"And I'm Jack Sinclair," said Jack. "We are all drinking lager. Would you like some?" He signalled to a waiter and introduced the rest of the table.

"Yes please," said Enid. "This your first time here?"

"Second. We came yesterday, but you all disappeared before Lucy could catch Daisy's eye."

"There was some sort of kerfuffle," said Enid vaguely. "Ooh, lovely lager. Thanks. I'm always parched after we finish a dance but we only get lager if a customer buys it for us because it's so posh."

"I was impressed to see it offered. Does they get it from the continent?"

"Wales, I think. Mr Arama was shouting on the telephone at the railway company the other day when it didn't come in. No wonder it's so dear." It was clear from Enid's manner that the lager might just as well have come from Europe.

While Lucy was struggling with her composure, Tufty Thomas leaned across the table to compliment the dancers on their routines. The girls both beamed with pleasure.

"Kitten Kaboodle," said Jack. "It's a clever name. Comes from the American phrase 'kit and caboodle', presumably. It suits the Black Cat club."

Enid nodded. "That's why they chose it. We used to be the Foxy Trotters, until there was a bit of trouble with the tax man. Well, Rose said it was tax. I think it was the police, myself. Rose only got off because she was friendly with Sergeant Roberts."

Jack continued to dispense his flow of chatter as if he was the idle playboy everybody thought. Lucy kept a gay smile on her face and eavesdropped on what Aidan and Daisy were saying.

"Basil Milcombe?" Aidan sounded furious. "You're telling me Basil Milcombe is the man you are frightened of?"

"Him and Mr Arama. They've both got money in the club. I don't know whether Rose is in with them or not, but they all want us to be friendly with the customers."

"By which you mean more than friendly, I take it?" Lucy hadn't heard her brother sound so angry since he'd gone for an inexperienced jockey who was using the whip with unnecessary force. He'd only been eleven at the time but had laid into the man like someone twice his age.

Daisy nodded unhappily. "It used to be just dancing and chatting - you expect that - but they opened up some rooms upstairs. That's why I want to get out of my contract."

"Why didn't you tell me?"

"I was ashamed," she whispered, so low Lucy could hardly make out the words. "I didn't want you to know what sort of outfit this was."

"I've got some of the money you need." He shot a glance past Lucy at where Jack's stream of nonsense had drawn Tufty and his friends into the conversation. "I'll borrow the rest from my brother-in-law-to-be."

"But then I won't have a job to help you pay it back. I just want things to be the way they were."

Lucy turned to them. "The club manager is oiling his way over," she said. "Time for a jolly discussion. What's your favourite, Daisy, the Charleston or the foxtrot?"

Daisy rallied bravely. "For dancing normally? Oh, the Charleston. It's got such lively moves."

"But the foxtrot has better tunes, don't you think?"

"Only because it's been around longer," said Aidan, catching on. "There must be three times as many foxtrot songs as Charleston. The bands have had time to refine them."

"Good evening, ladies and gentlemen. I hope you are enjoying all the amenities the Black Cat has to offer. Will you be taking supper?"

"Oh, I expect so, said Jack affably. "It was jolly good last night. Care to join us, ladies?"

"Ta very much," said Enid. "We've got one more routine, then we're free. Can't stay too long though. We need our beauty sleep considering how early we began practising today."

Youssif Arama resumed his glide around the room. Lucy watched him and saw with a start of surprise someone else she recognised, sitting by himself at a table.

"Mr Kent, yesterday, Mr Koivisto today," she said. "This really is the place to be."

"Mr Kent?" Enid looked alert and exchanged a glance with Daisy. "Lovely, isn't he? He's here quite a bit. I wouldn't mind if it was him, but it's always Rose he calls over."

This was sufficiently ambiguous for Lucy to want to probe further but she was interrupted.

Vilho Koivisto, feeling her gaze on him, glanced around, inclined his head and strolled across. "Good evening. Miss Kent mentioned your observations on the club's decor. I was curious to see for myself."

Because someone had copied his cupboards? Lucy put aside speculation, invited him to sit with them and introduced the others.

Jack, reading her mind as he so often did, smiled and shook hands. "Delighted to meet you. I'd be even more delighted if you asked Lucy for a dance. That way I can take a turn on the floor with Miss Bursall. Don't trust these shockers with my fiancée, I've known them all too long."

Mr Koivisto looked amused. "I would be enchanted."

"My brother will be wishing this was a waltz," observed Lucy as Aidan gave his hand to Daisy. "He'll have to wait until later. You can see why I thought of Miss Kent's room as soon as I saw the alcoves, can't you?"

"There is a striking resemblance, yes. The club is very stylishly put together."

Because they were dancing, Lucy was aware of a repressed emotion in him at variance with his light words. "I don't go to many nightclubs," she confided, "but Jack says the Black Cat is far better than a lot of them. This floor is lovely to dance on and the show numbers have all been super."

"No expense spared," he said shortly, and again Lucy thought there was something else behind the words. "Tell me, have you ever been to the Wentworth Gallery?"

"No," said Lucy, mystified. "Where is it?"

He smiled down at her with great charm. "It's not important. I simply wondered. These musicians are very good. They have certainly judged the clientele well. Thank you for taking pity on me. I was beginning to feel rather a misfit."

Because he was no longer a bright young thing? Because he was on his own? "I can't think why," she said. "You dance very proficiently."

"It is kind of you to say so. I am not sure my muscles will agree with you in the morning."

"The trick is not to think about the dance at all," said Lucy cunningly. "Then you will be more relaxed. Tell me how the designer has made a basement room look vaulted."

He laughed. "It is a matter of shadows and ratios," he began, and continued to enlighten her throughout the quickstep and the foxtrot that followed.

As the tune reached a triumphant climax, people cheered and laughingly dropped back into their seats. Enid and Daisy hurried out of the side door to get changed for the next routine.

Mr Koivisto eyes lingered on the concealed exit, then he turned to her with a smile. "It looks as though supper is arriving. I shall escort you back to your table, relieved to have got through the dance without treading on your toes. No doubt we will meet again on Monday in more conventional circumstances."

"Aren't you staying?"

"Thank you, no. I have already eaten and I was simply curious about the decor." He pulled out her chair and nodded to Jack. "My thanks for the loan of your fiancée."

Even as he turned away, Lucy was diving into her handbag for her notebook, desperate to jot down his words of wisdom before she forgot.

Two tables along, Basil Milcombe repeated the chorus to the last tune in a distressing falsetto. "I wonder, I wonder, I wonder, I wonder how I look when I'm asleep..."

Beside Lucy, Aidan growled that he'd love to show him.

"What, knock him out and take a photograph? Go home, Aidan, before you make an ass of yourself."

"I'll wait and see Daisy and Enid back. Besides, I'm hungry."

"Don't forget the last buses and trains leave at just gone midnight."

"I'm not likely to. We can't all afford taxis."

She gave him a level look. "If that's a dig at Jack, you can stop right now. I daresay we'll be taking the underground ourselves."

"Sorry." He continued to glower at Basil Milcombe's back. "Him of all people. God, I feel an idiot. He's made a right fool of me. That's the last time I run his errands, that's for sure."

Lucy put her notebook back in her bag. "Aidan, I'll lend you the money for Daisy. Jack will lend you the money for Daisy. But for goodness sake don't make a scene in front of a whole crowd of witnesses without hard-and-fast evidence to back it up. Here's the food. Eat, smile and enjoy the next routine."

Aidan's mouth set in a line. "I'll enjoy the dance. The rest might be a strain."

CHAPTER EIGHT

The management evidently approved of the dancers joining diners for supper. Jack noticed several of them adorning the tables once their final show-dance of the evening had finished. Rose herself was sitting with Basil Milcombe and the sleek businessmen. A couple of the older dancers were also at the table. Watching them without appearing to, Jack received the impression that whereas the dancers' interest in their companions was limited to the immediate future, between Rose and Milcombe there was a more practical, long-term air.

He continued to glance idly around the room. Youssif Arama was much in evidence helping out at the bar. Interestingly, a number of gentlemen discovered a need in themselves to drift over there to have an earnest word with him. It seemed to Jack that most of them palmed something before returning to their companions. He whistled softly to himself. Arama must be very sure there were no police on the premises tonight.

Lucy stretched up to whisper in his ear. "Basil is watching his every move, have you noticed? Daisy says he's got money in the club."

Jack smiled into her face as if she'd said something improper. There was a burst of laughter from further down the room. They both turned to see Theo Nicholson jump up and have a word with the band leader. Moments later, the strains of *Ain't She Sweet* was filling the room and Julie and Amanda Lester were giving their own exhibition dance. On the second repeat, Theo and Hubert joined them in what was obviously a rehearsed move. When the song finished, all four sat down, happily out of breath, to a round of applause.

Jack grinned at Lucy. "Hubert was telling me the engaged couples have taken apartments in the same building for after the wedding. I don't think marriage is going to make that much difference to the twins' lifestyle."

"I can't imagine them ever being any different. They'll have to adapt if they start families, though."

Enid looked up from her supper, having only caught part of the conversation. "You don't want to have a baby," she said in all seriousness. "Not if you can help it. Does terrible things to your figure."

"I'd like children," said Daisy. "Two boys and two girls."

Jack laughed at Aidan's startled expression.

"Then you'd better all cut off home so my brother can get on with studying for his next set of exams," said Lucy. "Doctors with hopeful families need a lot of sixpences coming through the door of the surgery."

Other people were already departing, though the band were evidently prepared to play dance tunes until the small hours. Milcombe stood up and shook the hands of his companions, leaving them at the table with the dancers. Rose moved smoothly over to the bar where she exchanged a few words with Arama before slipping through the side door.

"Hurry up, Enid," said Daisy. We'll miss the last bus if we aren't careful."

Enid got to her feet good-naturedly. "Driver will wait. He usually does. He's got a daughter our age and he says he wouldn't like to think of her having to walk home alone.

Let me grab a few of these matchbooks for our Cecil. They only came in today and he smokes so much they'll save him a good few coppers. Very posh, aren't they?"

Daisy glanced quickly at the bar. "Quick then, while Mr Arama isn't watching. They're supposed to be for customers."

"What about us?" Lucy asked Jack, sotto voce. "Seen all you need to see?"

"I've seen as much as I'm likely to be allowed to see, which isn't quite the same thing, but will have to do."

Fate, however, in the shape of Amanda Lester, had other ideas. "Jack," she cried as they passed their table, "we've been here all evening and you haven't asked either of us to dance yet."

"Couldn't get a look in," he said, slipping back into his amiable playboy persona. "No slight intended. Have you met my fiancée? Lucy, these reprobates are Julie and Amanda Lester, Theo Nicholson and Hubert Jarmaine. The gentlemen are both viscounts, though you wouldn't know it to look at them."

"Oh, I would," replied Lucy, smiling shyly, "I've seen you in the society pages and picture papers. Did you devise that dance yourself? It was awfully good."

"Thank you," replied Amanda. "Aren't the band dreamy? We've got a whole stack of their records at home. I couldn't believe it when we got here and realised they were the house orchestra. That's Harry Bidgood himself at the piano. We're going to do a Yale Blues dance later. Harry said he's looking forward to playing it for us. We've already bought tickets for the gala night next week."

Jack exchanged a look with Hubert. "Yes, I got caught for those too."

Julie Lister patted the chair next to her. "Come and sit down, Lucy. Where's Jack been keeping you? He's such a dark horse. We were all so surprised when we saw the announcement."

Jack opened his mouth to reply, but Lucy was before him.

"My father owns a racing stable in Newmarket," she explained, with a roguish twinkle up at him, "and then one day we bumped into each other in a Corner House away from all the horses and distractions and simply never stopped talking."

Which was all true, but not necessarily how they had actually met and fallen in love. Clever Lucy. "Nice smokescreen," said Jack when they finally got away.

"I can't believe they didn't recognise me," said Lucy. "I must remember never, ever to wear Phoebe's pink and silver when I'm anywhere near them. We've missed all the last transport as well. It'll have to be a taxi. What a good thing Aidan isn't here to see it."

Even as she spoke, a cab slowed down next to them. "Do you need a ride somewhere, guv?" asked their driver from earlier.

"Hello! Yes, Edgar Mansions, please. That's a stroke of luck," said Jack.

"Happy accident, guv. Got turned around on Oxford Street, coppers everywhere, so had to double back."

"Lucky for us," said Lucy, getting into the cab with a sigh of relief. "Going out with you every night is exhausting. I'm not sure my feet are ever going to recover."

"I'm beginning to wonder about the lifestyle myself," agreed Jack. "I could sleep for a week." But not, sadly, until after he'd written a report for Uncle Bob on what he'd seen and learned tonight while the facts and impressions were fresh in his mind.

Vilho was woken on Sunday morning by the peal of the telephone bell. He rolled out of bed to answer it, wincing at his protesting muscles. "Hello?"

"Vilho, I'm coming back early. I need to talk to you."

His mind snapped alert. "Here? Or Fitzroy Square?"

There was a pause.

"Christina? Are you there?"

"I'm here. I'll come to you. Goodbye."

The connection clicked off. Vilho bathed, shaved and put the coffee on, assailed by a hundred hurrying thoughts.

Lucy lay in bed listening to the early morning church bells. It was one of the things she loved about London, the way they all combined from a dozen different parishes to float over the rooftops announcing a day of rest and reflection.

"What are you thinking?" asked Jack's sleepy voice next to her.

"That I should go upstairs to Phoebe's darkroom and develop the photographs from last night. The sooner I get the prints to the *Chronicle* the sooner I'll be paid."

"Practical, but not romantic."

"And while I'm doing that, you can go to Lower Belgrave Street and bring my typewriter back. I've got no end of useful stuff from Mr Koivisto to type up."

"It won't look like an office without a typewriter."

"Then stop off at your own place on the way and pick up yours."

"Hen-pecked, and we aren't even married yet," he said mournfully. "Ah well, it won't harm to remind Vickers of my existence before he starts looking for another position. Do you want first use of the bathroom or shall..."

He was interrupted by a sharp rapping on the flat door.

Alarm swept through Lucy. "Something must be wrong at home," she said, scrambling out of bed and pulling on her robe. "Or with Aidan. No one else would come to the door this early." She dashed out into her hallway.

Jack thudded after her, his hand coming hard over her shoulder to hold the door shut as she reached it. "Ask who it is," he murmured.

Fresh terror. Lucy glanced at his alert, focused face, her heart banging. Lord, he was dangerous. "Who is it?" she said in a high voice.

"Bob Curtis. Tell that nephew of mine I don't know why I'm bothering to sub his bachelor rooms when he's never there."

Lucy sagged in relief. Behind her, Jack also relaxed, and motioned for her to step aside. He opened the door a crack. One glimpse and he slipped off the safety chain to let his uncle in.

Curtis nodded approval at the precautions and walked into the sitting room where he threw himself into a chair and dropped the newspaper he was carrying on to the table. He looked tired and rumpled and clearly hadn't shaved since the previous day.

"Tell me it's nothing to do with me," said Lucy, "and I'll make us a pot of tea."

"It's *probably* nothing to do with you," he said, passing a hand over his face.

"Give me two minutes to get dressed," said Jack. "A fellow feels such a fool discussing matters of state in his nightwear."

"Two minutes," agreed his uncle, leaning his head back against the chair rest and closing his eyes. "It isn't matters of state."

Lucy looked from one to the other and withdrew to investigate the contents of the bread bin.

A quarter of an hour later, fortified by tea and toast, Jack said, "Have you come to tell us to stay away from the Black Cat club?"

"Very close. You were there last night." It was a statement, not a question.

"I told you we would be," replied Jack. "I've written a report. There are a couple of points of interest."

"Good. I might need it. Did you talk to Basil Milcombe at all?"

"Milcombe? No, we may have nodded across the room but nothing more. It was very busy, people were sticking to their own groups in the main. Why?"

"Because at just gone midnight he met an untimely death under the wheels of the No 14 bus."

"Basil Milcombe?" said Lucy in surprise. "Never. He was in revoltingly high spirits when he left, but he certainly wasn't drunk enough to walk in front of a bus."

"When would that have been?"

"Ten to twelve? Twelve o'clock? Something like that."

"Did you actually see him leave?"

"No, we were still on the dance floor. I saw him go up the stairs."

Jack was watching his uncle narrowly. "I wouldn't have said he was bosky. My impression was that he'd had a successful evening and was looking forward to whatever tomorrow might bring, in which he was evidently wrong. I don't suppose many people will be shedding tears."

"My father and Douglas will," Lucy pointed out. "He's got horses with them. Who's going to pay the training and livery costs?"

"Next of kin. Milcombe's father, at a guess. Why do you come into it, Uncle Bob?"

"Because according to the bystanders, his last word before life was extinguished was 'pushed'."

"He was pushed? It wasn't an accident?" Jack pursed his lips in a whistle. "That does put a different complexion on it. He had enemies, of course. You can't live his sort of life without making some. What happened? You said there were bystanders. Did anyone see him go under?"

Curtis snorted with derision. "They all saw. Unfortunately, as is the case with eye-witnesses, they all saw something different. There was a woman next to him. No, there was a man. No, no, he was on his own. You name a combination, someone saw it. One fairly reliable onlooker saw two men standing close together, waiting to cross. Both wearing overcoats and hats."

"Very useful."

"There's something else," said Lucy. "You smirked when Jack said Basil Milcombe's father was next of kin."

"What sharp eyes you have, niece-to-be. See what you make of this. A luckless minion at Somerset House, whom I diverted from his Sunday devotions this morning, has confirmed that Basil Milcombe got married two years ago."

"He's wrong," Lucy said positively. "Milcombe doesn't look married. He doesn't act married. He never refers to a wife. Everyone talks about him as the eternal club man."

"Until today, that was my impression too. Nevertheless, two years ago he tied the knot with a Miss Rose Gertrude Smith at St Giles Cripplegate. His man was a witness. Is there any more tea in that pot?" Chief Inspector Curtis settled back in his chair with quiet satisfaction at the stupefied look on their faces.

"Help yourself," said Lucy. She put together this astonishing information with the interaction she had noticed last night. "Rose Gertrude Smith? You're not telling us Basil Milcombe was married to Rose Garden, the leader of the Kitten Kaboodle troupe at the Black Cat club?"

"Formerly known as the Foxy Trotters. That is what she told my officer in the early hours of the morning, shortly before demanding Milcombe's personal effects."

"Oh, of course, the club would still have been open," said Jack. "You didn't give them to her?"

"We aren't amateurs, nephew, no matter how the writers of detective novels like to portray us." He winked at Lucy. "No, she thinks we're still waiting for proof. It hasn't occurred to her we don't hand over useful items to possible suspects just like that."

Lucy was bewildered, remembering the redhead twining around Paul Kent, her rapid assessment of Jack on Friday. "It seems impossible. She didn't act married any more than he did."

Jack was watching his uncle. "What happened two years ago?" he asked.

Curtis grinned. "Well done. Two years ago, Miss Gertie Smith, a small-time dancer with big ideas and a flexible attitude towards the law, inherited a flourishing stationer's shop from her old dad. She promptly sold it."

"Ready cash would always be an attraction for Milcombe," said Jack. "It must have come in handy for his Guildford gaming hell enterprise. We wondered at the time who was bankrolling it. I don't remember ever seeing her down there though."

"Yes, but why would she marry him?" said Lucy. "What would she get out of it? Security? Was she having a child?"

Curtis snorted. "Simpler than that. The last will and testament of Jeremiah 'Hell Fire' Smith stipulated that his daughter would only inherit the shop on the condition she was married and had renounced her immoral life."

"Ugh," said Lucy. "Control from beyond the grave. So she cast around for a suitable business partner. I'm not sure I would have picked Basil Milcombe even if I was in a hurry."

"She must have driven some sort of bargain with him. They appear to have shared similar attitudes. Milcombe's solicitor tells me the lady is insisting on complete anonymity while they sort out his estate. Milcombe Senior is said to be apoplectic, unless that was fury at being roused so early on a Sunday with the news."

"Basil has been the black sheep of the family for ever,"

said Jack. "If his father isn't even going to inherit his horses after years of putting up with his exploits, he'll wonder what life has against him."

"*Was* he pushed?" asked Lucy.

"I imagine so, if that's what he claimed. Leaving aside the fact that people don't in general fall under buses, even if they've had a few, he's the sort who would know and as Jack said, he's certainly made enemies in the past. Pity he died before elaborating."

"You have been busy," observed Jack. "Soho nightlife, Somerset House, solicitors and country squires all before ten o'clock. How did you know to start at the Black Cat club?"

"Let me guess," said Lucy. "He had a Black Cat club ticket in his pocket."

Curtis grinned. "That also only happens in detective novels."

"Were you keeping Milcombe under observation?" asked Jack.

"We were keeping the *club* under observation. Your 'ebony kitten' advertisement, remember? It seemed a good idea in case any of our known suppliers took the notion into their heads to pay a visit. That's why I was still at the Yard instead of being comfortably tucked up in bed. One of my men saw Milcombe go in and noted it down. He's a bright lad because he also suggested we follow up a suspicious young woman who was hanging around outside and kept blocking his view by taking photographs of random guests going into the club."

"They were carefully selected guests, I'll have him know," said Lucy without rancour. "Going back to Basil Milcombe, the conversation I saw between him and Rose looked brisk and businesslike. No flashing looks or hissed threats. No emotion at all, really."

"Wives are always top of the list when it comes to

motive," said Curtis. "She's a hard-boiled young woman, that's for sure. She told me to my face she wasn't going to say a word until she sees her solicitor. And by that time he'll have coached her, or she'll have coached herself, and I won't get a thing out of her."

Lucy exchanged a look with Jack. "That's not surprising, considering what else we think was going on there."

"Apart from the drugs?"

"Soliciting," said Jack briefly. "Immoral earnings. There are rooms upstairs. Arama and Rose are definitely complicit. Milcombe knew all about it. Last night he'd brought a party of gentlemen along especially to show them a good time and he left without them. Additionally, one of the dancers we talked to thinks he has a stake in the club, which would be worth your following up. Oh..." A look of enlightenment came over his face. "Oh, I wonder... Yes, that would explain why George Forrest is unshackling himself from the Black Cat club."

Curtis sat up alertly. "Forrest is what?"

"Selling out or calling in the loan at a guess. I only found out yesterday when he mentioned it at the bridge table. He cited a disagreement over policy. He isn't generally fussy about where profits come from, but he does hold strong views on the purity of women."

Curtis scribbled in the notebook that was suddenly in his hand. "Useful to know. Everyone has their line in the sand. I'll get someone to look into it. Good excuse for a search warrant for the club. Returning to the accident, can you remember anyone who left the dance floor around the same time as Milcombe?"

"Quite a lot. Most of the last buses go at midnight." Lucy faltered with the appalling realisation that it had indeed been Milcombe's last bus.

"I have the list from the visitor's book," said Curtis noncommittally. "I saw your brother's name there. Jack mentioned they knew each other."

Lucy suppressed her flare of panic, remembering Aidan's fury last night. "We've all known Basil Milcombe for years. Aidan's run a couple of errands for him recently. He might have seen something, yes. He left with two of the dancers, Daisy Brickett and Enid Bursall. They room in a hostel together and he was seeing them home. He has an understanding with Daisy." She braced herself for more questions, but after a thoughtful glance at her, Curtis didn't continue.

Jack frowned. "We were delayed by the Lester twins, but I'll cast my mind back and write down as many people as I can remember."

"I'd be glad of it. We're contacting the ones in the visitors' book who we think left around that time, but it's shocking how unreliable people's memories are after a few cocktails."

"About Rose not talking to you..." said Jack.

Curtis met his eyes. "Got an idea?"

"Maybe. Someone who sells her dear old dad's business as soon as he shuffles off his mortal coil is a lot more fond of money than she is of sentiment. Lucy, are any of the horses Milcombe had with your father or brother likely to be within my reach?"

Relieved that they'd dropped the subject of Aidan, Lucy grinned at him. "Oh, you are clever. Yes, the mare Rick mentioned. Flotsam. The young one in foal for the first time. You could make an offer on her. Rose will snap your hand off if she's as greedy as she looks, especially if Rick gives Flotsam a poor prognosis for surviving the birth. I'll ring this morning once they've finished the early routine. They ought to be told about Milcombe anyway."

Curtis raised his eyebrows. "And just how are you going to explain suddenly buying a horse?"

Jack grinned. "Wedding present for Lucy. She took a fancy to the mare some time ago. Naturally, I trust the in-laws implicitly as I know nothing about horseflesh."

"Genius," murmured Lucy. "You'll have to meet Rose in person to sign the contract and pay over the requisite number of guineas. Jack Sinclair has never yet failed to get women eating out of his hand."

Curtis nodded judiciously. "The sooner the better, before she thinks to put a guard on her tongue. Speed is of the essence here. How good a dissembler is your brother, Lucy? If he could ring Milcombe's rooms today with Jack's offer to buy the horse, Milcombe's man will pass the message to Rose. He knew all about the marriage, having been a witness at the wedding. My inspector is there now, going over the place for anything in the light of a clue. She's already tried to take possession, but he said he needed official proof of the marriage and shut the door in her face."

Jack leaned back with satisfaction. "Thus she will be nicely frustrated and in the mood to act instantly on the chance of a sale. I might even get to commiserate with her on her loss as soon as tomorrow."

CHAPTER NINE

On his way to his own flat, Jack kept his usual watch about him. It was such an ingrained habit that when he recognised what he was doing, he came to an abrupt halt, revisited by the revulsion he'd felt earlier when he stopped Lucy opening her own front door in case there was danger on the other side. The awareness that because of his way of life, because of his job, *she* was going to have to learn caution, *she* would need to be suspicious every moment of the day. He walked on soberly, the knowledge sticking in his craw. This was why he'd never let himself get deeply involved with a woman before.

Not true, Jack. You didn't get involved because none of them were Lucy.

Despite himself, a smile tugged at his lips. Her energy. Her quick-wittedness. Her independent spirit. The way her impish grin melted his vital organs. His inner voice had it right. Once he'd admitted he loved her, the end result had never been in doubt. So get on with the task in hand, Jack, and tell her what she needs to know as you go along. The decision cheered him up so much he even managed to put up with Vickers' implicit assumption that before leaving for Lower Belgrave Street he would be changing into the fresh set of clothes laid ready on the bed.

The building was quiet. Nobody was working on a Sunday. It didn't follow that it would remain quiet. Jack stood in the doorway of the Consolidated Cocoa office. Nothing seemed to have changed since yesterday. They needn't have been in such a rush to leave after all. He drew closer to the careless fan of unopened envelopes. Most contained single sheets of paper. He guessed they would be similar to his own enquiry, requesting information about the *'low stakes good returns'* advertisement. Three or four were thicker. Reports, perhaps? Information on speculation? Or nice gossipy family letters to give him an idea of what Trelawny was actually like? Very, very gently he slid two away from their fellows and into his pocket.

By the time Christina tapped lightly at Vilho's door, his sitting room was rich with the smell of good coffee and her favourite biscuits were on a plate. He took her coat, reflecting that he had rarely seen her looking so determined.

"What's the matter?" he asked. "Is it Garth?"

She was surprised into a laugh. "For once, no. My father is as well as an inadvisably-rich dinner and a late night can make him. The problem is Paul. I am almost too angry and too ashamed of him to speak."

Vilho let out a breath. This was going to be simpler than he had feared. "I also have information about Paul. Will it make easier for you if I tell you I have proof that he copied my designs for the Wentworth Gallery and used them for the Black Cat club? He requested the plans from the archive and was a week in returning them. I went there last night. There can be no doubt, Christina. I am sorry."

She shut her eyes briefly, as if she'd been expecting something of the sort but it had hit her anyway. "Don't be," she said. "He sold a conservatory design to James and

97

Emily Durban that was near-identical to the one we did for the Lucases of Westmoor Place. It did not go through the company books. There are other blueprints in his plan chest at Radlett. All copies. I suppose he kept them there to be safe."

Vilho gave her arm a sympathetic squeeze and busied himself with the coffee. "It is some comfort to know none of our competitors are stealing our designs."

She gave a bitter laugh. "We could deal with that. There are laws and the police to do it for us. Paul, borrowing here and there from the company archives without putting the profits back into the firm, is something rather different. He has also been asking Papa to release some capital, supposedly to build prototypes of your modular homes."

Vilho stared. "He doesn't like my homes. He said they would never prosper here."

"Papa said the same. He advised him to first find a builder who would countenance the idea, then he might think about it." She sipped her coffee and nibbled one of the biscuits.

"Marion is very expensive," said Vilho eventually. "I know she has money of her own, but it would not surprise me that they might find themselves in difficulties."

"Marion is expensive, the girls all have school fees and Paul never considers pulling in his own horns to balance his household expenses. His idea of economy is to order a new coat to delay his tailor billing him for the last one. I can almost hear him explaining it is good for business to show a prosperous face to the world. And as he will no doubt tell us, many architects also work privately."

"But they don't patch together their colleague's designs and pass it off as their own work." Vilho looked at her face, downbent over her coffee cup. "Why else did you come back early? Why did you need to see me?"

She smiled faintly. "To talk over what we should do.

And... and because I cannot say this next part to anyone else." She took a deep breath. "The private work wasn't all I found in his plan chest. His student portfolio was there too."

"He kept that? It must be twenty years ago now."

"Vilho, it contained *my* ideas and designs. Flights of fancy. Beautiful twiddles. Things I'd tried out, but that Papa had said would never sell."

Vilho had thought he was calm, but at her words anger exploded in him. He realised it had been there all along. "Even then he was stealing from you? That's unforgivable. Christina, I swear I didn't know. How could I? I had never seen any of your work at that stage. My God, what colossal nerve. He would have been expelled from the School of Architecture. He would never have got his diploma."

Christina studied her cup. "It explains why he was so uncharacteristically quiet about his designs. Do you remember how he threw himself into the company, faithfully following Papa's direction? A model son."

"I remember." *I thought he had turned over a new leaf. I thought it was a challenge to me.*

"I imagine," Christina continued, "when he was suddenly surrounded by other bright students, he found himself out of his depth and it shocked him. Everything had always come easily to him before. He took success for granted."

"I was swept away by him, I admit," said Vilho ruefully. "Paul had enormous presence in those days. I had never in my life met anyone with so much confidence. He was head and shoulders above the rest of the class in that respect."

"But not in ideas. So he used mine." She looked up. "Did Papa know? He had certainly seen my work."

Vilho shrugged, helpless. "How can we tell? What I do know is that Garth has always had a blind spot where Paul is concerned."

She nodded, then made an impatient gesture. "In any case, it is too late to bring up something that happened so long ago. My father would have to listen to the present evidence, but how can I tell him Paul is reusing company designs to finance his own lifestyle? It would kill him."

"Garth may already suspect and finds it easier to ignore it than to ask. He sees the company reports and listens to his neighbours' conversations after all. But we *do* tackle Paul. The designs belong to the company. It is fraud, Christina."

She lifted her chin. "We will confront him on Tuesday. Fraser and Timmins are coming in tomorrow to sign off the redesign of their offices. I would prefer my brother to be his usual gregarious self until the ink is dry on the contract."

He smiled. "Practical as ever. I agree."

There was no sound from Lucy's apartment when Jack let himself in. He replaced the typewriter on her table and saw her note. *Developing. Won't be long.*

He chuckled, slipped on a pair of thin cotton gloves and took the two letters addressed to Consolidated Cocoa out of his pocket. He looked at them for some time before gently inserting the handle of a spoon in the space between the top of one envelope and the gummed flap. Working carefully he got it open and drew out the contents. He stared, dumfounded. It was not a letter. The reason for the bulk was four Bank of England five-pound notes. There was a sheet of cheap paper folded around them with a few scrawled words. It read *£20 for unit shares in the name of Matthew Stone.*

Jack wrote the sentence down in his pocketbook, then replaced the money and wrapper in the envelope. A dab of gum would see to the seal. He turned his attention to the second envelope. This time, six five-pound notes fell out. A different hand requested unit shares in the name of Mark Diamond.

Investors were sending Trelawny wads of money in the post! They must be very sure of him. Jack wrote this message down too and considered his next move. He would have had no compunction about keeping letters or reports, trusting to Trelawny blaming the postal system for them going astray, but these treasury notes represented people's hard-earned savings. Much as he had doubts about the dividends coming from returns on cocoa investments, he couldn't simply steal the money. He would have to replace the envelopes in the Consolidated Cocoa office or return them to the senders.

Returning them would be the kindest option. It was also likely to be the most practical as Trelawny may well have gone into the office by now to deal with his post. There was a snag, though, in that the senders' addresses weren't on either the letters or the envelopes. He would have to extract them from Trelawny's records. And that would have to wait until Lucy had developed the photographs she had taken yesterday.

Jack put the affair aside for the moment. He was accustomed to working on several projects at once. There were other articles he could be getting on with, an excoriating treatise on unscrupulous landlords forcing tenants out by increasing their rent for a start. He opened his brief case and delved inside.

Leaving the prints pegged up in Phoebe's small room to dry, Lucy entered her own sitting room and surveyed Jack affectionately as he sat hunched over his notepad in concentration, papers spread around him, one hand rumpling his dark hair as the other travelled swiftly across the page.

"I know you're there," he said without looking up.

"We're going to need a larger table," she commented. *And another wardrobe, and a second hat stand.*

"We might need a larger apartment. Are there any bigger ones in this building? I like it here."

A frisson of pure love ran through her. There he went again, talking about the future as if it was real. "We could ask the concierge," she said.

"Before I forget, there was a letter from my mother at the flat reminding me about cousin Bridget's art show. It's opening tomorrow and the family is expected to turn up and support her. Early evening, so we won't need to be there very long. How do you feel about it?"

Lucy's stomach plunged. "Terrified."

He grinned at her in sympathy. "But willing?"

She took a deep breath. "I'll brace myself." She smiled bravely back and moved around the table to type up a nice gossipy column for 'Society Snippets'.

"I can post that tomorrow, if you like. I'm going back to Lower Belgrave Street. It would save you having to remember it before work."

"Thanks. I hope you discover what Trelawny is up to. I do worry about Miss Reed entrusting her savings to him."

"She's not alone. I found actual banknotes in two of his letters. I need to return them. Did you develop the photographs you took of the lists of subscribers?"

"Yes, I'll bring them down when they are dry."

He grinned. "Nice this, working together."

It was. Lucy finished her column and applied herself to the telephone, firstly to acquaint her father with the news that one of his owners would be taking no further interest in his horses and then to tell Douglas the same thing and to say Jack wanted to buy Flotsam as a wedding present for her. "We saw Basil last night and Jack mentioned it to him. He was amenable but I don't want the sale to get lost in a tangle of lawyers. Can you ring his rooms straight away, Douglas, pretending you haven't heard, and ask his man to pass the message on that you are worried about Flotsam's health and if Basil still wants to sell her, he'd better do it fast?"

Her elder brother's voice was blunt. "That's ridiculous, Lucy. What sort of chap recommends an ailing horse to his sister? Basil would see through it in an instant."

"Basil is dead, Doug," repeated Lucy patiently. "His heirs won't think anything of it at all. Give his man the message and Jack's address. He'll pass it on to the right person. What would you say she was worth? Two hundred guineas? I can't bear the thought of her being sacrificed for the sake of the foal and you know that's what will happen if it's left to accountants. This way you can continue to look after her."

That got through to him. He replied gruffly that he'd do what he could.

"Will he pull it off?" asked Jack.

"Oh yes. He cares about all his mares. He doesn't show it, but he suffered horribly during the war, breeding horses to ship to Flanders that he would never see again."

"And yet he got on with a louse like Milcombe?"

"I didn't like Basil Milcombe but he was a different man in the stables," said Lucy fairly. "Horses were the one thing he was passionate about. Doug respected that. Meanwhile, what about Aidan? Should I let him know? There isn't a telephone at his lodgings, so I'll have to write."

"Can't hurt," said Jack, "though Uncle Bob's team will probably have done it by the time he gets the letter. I get the impression they are going to be asking everyone who was at the Black Cat around midnight what time they left and whether they noticed anything."

"Aidan was seeing the girls home," she said quickly. "He'd have been with them." But he had left at roughly the same time as Basil Milcombe and he had been furious with him. She wrote a carefully informative letter, hoping her brother would be able to read the warning between the lines.

"This is odd," Jack said later, frowning over the photographs of the notebook while she chose which prints to send to the *Chronicle*.

"What is?"

"The two men that I was going to return the Consolidated Cocoa stake money to aren't here, and yet they must be existing customers because neither of them gave addresses."

"Perhaps they were only potential subscribers. They may have written initial query letters as you did, and assumed Trelawny would keep their addresses. He must file those separately."

"Yes, they could be in the card index. Bother."

"Hopefully you'll get a chance to check tomorrow. Trelawny must go out for lunch at some point. You might be able to nip in and do a bit of sleuthing."

CHAPTER TEN

Jack arrived at his new office on Monday morning at what the majority of his acquaintance would consider a frankly unbelievable hour. He bought a selection of newspapers from the stand on the corner and settled down to read them with the door ajar so he would know as soon as the adjoining office was opened up.

Milcombe had made the news, he noticed, tucked away on an inner page under the headline 'Death of Club Man' with a statement from a shaken bus driver saying that he simply stepped out in front of him and it shouldn't be allowed.

"Poor blighter," muttered Jack. "He's going to recall that moment every time he sits behind the steering wheel."

He skimmed the rest of the news and then went through the advertisements, noting anything odd or unlikely that might be worth following up.

Noises drifted up the stairwell, heralding the arrival of office workers, fresh from their weekend break. Presently he heard brisk footsteps and saw a middle-aged woman walk past his door, slowing as she hunted in her handbag for a key.

He heard the click of a lock, then there was an "Oh," of surprise.

He ambled into the corridor. "Good morning. I was beginning to think I was the only person on this floor."

The woman gave him a frosty smile. Evidently she didn't believe in frivolous chatter before starting work. "It is generally quiet first thing. People come and go later. I'm only here twice week. Or I should be." She looked around the room in a disapproving manner.

"Is something wrong?"

"Inconvenient. My employer hasn't left my usual list of tasks."

"Perhaps it is in a drawer. Sorry, I should have introduced myself. Shocking manners. The name's Sinclair. I work at Elljay, next door."

She gave him a slight nod. "Mrs Antrobus. Mondays and Thursdays, nine o'clock until four o'clock." She crossed to the table and looked in the drawers. Evidently there was nothing there that she didn't expect to see. "This is all most odd. Mr Trelawny must have gone away for the weekend. The post hasn't been dealt with, no instructions left for me and no wages. It's not what I'm used to at all."

"Jolly bad form," agreed Jack sympathetically. "Can't you carry on from where you finished last time? Surely your employer said something about the plan for this week."

"I didn't see him. I rarely do. He is a very busy gentleman, which is why he requires clerical help. He leaves me the list of tasks and the day's wages and I get on with it. I could very easily continue with the normal schedule, but not without guaranteed payment. Four shillings is four shillings. I can't afford to give anyone a day for free no matter how agreeable they are, and so I told him when he engaged me. I'll leave a note to say I'll return on Thursday. Some of my other regulars will be glad of the offer of extra hours."

"Good for you," Jack applauded. "What does he look

like, this governor of yours? I'll tell him you were here if he shows up."

She glanced at him witheringly. "Mr Trelawny will know I was here from the note."

"Oh yes, foolish of me. I daresay you are right and he's been delayed. Nothing more likely when you think about it." Jack withdrew to his room, listening to the acerbic rattle of typewriter keys, followed by Mrs Antrobus locking up and taking herself off.

He considered what she had told him. First, that she rarely saw her employer. That indicated to Jack that Trelawny was in full-time employment elsewhere and called in to Consolidated Cocoa during the evenings or at weekends. Second, that he was always busy. In other words, when he was here he was rushed. It could therefore be that his job was at some distance, leaving him limited time to get across London, give Mrs Antrobus her instructions and depart. Third, and most important to Jack's mind, was Mrs Antrobus considering Trelawny the sort of gentleman who went away for weekends. The majority of people in her situation would assume their employer was ill.

This made Trelawny healthy, of smart appearance and with an air of ease and good humour. Jack's circle was full of many such gentlemen. It was an addictive way of life. He could quite see that having hit on an ingenious method of augmenting his income, Trelawny would be prepared to pay a clerk eight bob a week to do the donkey work of writing out the cheques, while he simply spent an hour a day keeping the business ticking over.

Why Belgravia? For the good business address, presumably. Was there another reason?

Jack picked up Lucy's envelope for the *Chronicle*. He rather thought now might be an excellent time to visit the local post office and familiarise himself with the locker arrangement for post office box numbers.

There was an air of cheerfulness at Paul Kent Architects when Lucy arrived on Monday morning. Partly this was Miss Hodge happily saying what a lovely weekend she'd had and reporting that Smithy was very much better, nearly her old self again. But there was something else, thought Lucy, something indefinable.

Miss Reed enlightened her. "You will need to make extra tea for the meeting in Mr Kent's room this afternoon. They are signing a new contract," she added with a sort of possessive pride.

"If the clients don't change their mind," murmured Mrs Corrigan, looking worried.

"They won't. Mr Kent is in very good spirits. That's always an indication things are going well."

"I don't see how you can tell what his mood is," said Miss Hodge. "All we heard was him saying good morning to the receptionist."

"I assure you, when you have worked here for as long as I have, a few words and the tone of voice is all that is needed."

"How long *have* you been here?" asked Lucy hastily.

"You were already with the company when I was here before the war," said Mrs Corrigan. "I've always been grateful that you put a word in for me when I needed to come back again."

Miss Reed smiled graciously at her. "I was very pleased to. I've worked here since leaving school. I took a Pitman's course and joined from there. Mr Garth Kent was head of the practice in those days. Miss Kent has always been articled to him, but Mr Paul Kent only joined as a full partner after he obtained his diploma."

Miss Kent had trained under her father? She hadn't gone to a school of architecture like her brother? That was a useful nugget of information for Lucy's research notes. "And Mr Koivisto?" she asked, more to keep Miss Reed talking than anything else. She could have kicked herself for not realising before that the older woman might be a fund of knowledge about what went into the making of an architect. *Lesson for Lucy: never underestimate the company typists.*

"He started as a draughtsman as soon as Mr Paul Kent introduced him to his father. They were students together, even though Mr Koivisto was a little older. Mr Garth Kent took quite a fancy to him. At first it was during the vacations, then permanently once he obtained his diploma."

That sounded a more normal route. Miss Reed joining the company straight from school though... Lucy was both astounded and horrified. No wonder she was loyal to the firm if she'd never known anything different. Lucy stole a covert glance at her. What was she, forty-five? Not so very much older than Miss Kent. It made sense that she would have a special affection for Paul Kent. She must have been very inexperienced when she first knew him, susceptible to a young gentleman with a laughing manner and audacious ways. How had she felt when Mr Kent married and started a family? Jack had told her Mrs Kent had been a wealthy, sought-after socialite. Perhaps Miss Reed considered it only fitting that Mr Kent had won her hand. Certainly she seemed content with her narrow life: her work here, her gramophone records, her books changed very week at the circulating library.

Calm of mind, all passion spent. Milton's line came into Lucy's head, making her shudder. All passion spent at forty-five. That really was an appalling thought.

"Are you quite well, Miss Brown?"

Lucy jumped as Miss Reed's voice intruded into her thoughts. She swallowed. "I'm so sorry, was I wool gathering? I did wonder if I was coming down with a cold yesterday, but I'm sure I'm all right really." She applied herself to typing up a costing of the materials required to convert a ballroom into a self-contained apartment. This, she reflected ruefully, was why she was a novelist, not making a career out of being an efficient, purposeful typist. Her mind would keep distracting her by considering what made people the way they were. All the same, she had an overwhelming longing to feel Jack's arms around her, to know all *her* passion wasn't spent, to know she wasn't alone.

As if she had conjured him up, Jack was waiting outside when it was her turn to go for lunch.

"Hello," she said, inordinately pleased to see him. "Mrs Corrigan, this is my fiancé, Mr Sinclair. Have you come to buy me lunch, Jack?"

"I have." Jack turned with a smile to Mrs Corrigan. "Would you like to join us? You would be most welcome."

"That's very kind, but I don't live far away." She gave a small laugh. "How silly of me, I thought the gentleman who was here on Saturday must be your fiancé, even though he seemed rather too young."

Lucy grinned. "That was my brother, Aidan. I frequently think he is too young."

"I hope she wasn't just being polite," said Jack as the older woman hurried off. "Was she really going home for lunch?"

Lucy linked her arm in his. "She really was. Is the Lyons all right with you? I only have an hour. Why are you here? Have you found out something to do with Consolidated Cocoa?"

"In a way. Mr Trelawny employs a lady clerk twice a week to make out the cheques and type the envelopes, is rarely there during the day, and is the sort who goes away for the weekend. Oh, and Elljay Associates is now the proud possessor of a Post Office box number."

"That's very businesslike. I hope it is worth it. Would

you like me to type some random letters to send us?"

"That was also in my mind. Here you are, I wrote the address down. I'll send a couple myself as well." He passed her a slip of paper. "The real reason I came, apart from missing you, was to ask if your Miss Reed described Mr Trelawny. I'm haunted by the thought I might pass him on the stairs and have no idea who he is."

Lucy cast her mind back. "She hasn't, but I'll try to think of a reason to ask."

"I have full confidence in you."

Accordingly, once she had hung up her hat and coat after a most satisfactory lunchtime interlude, Lucy put on a brightly deferential smile and said, "I mentioned your ten-pound units to my fiancé, Miss Reed. He was very interested. He says he knows a Mr Trelawny who is a big, red-bearded Cornishman and he *thinks* he is something in the City. Might that be the same gentleman?"

"I'm afraid I wouldn't know. I only communicate with Mr Trelawny by post. I have never met him in person."

Lucy's mouth fell open. "You sent him ten pounds *in the post?*"

"Really, Miss Brown, I wrote a cheque made out to Consolidated Cocoa. Anything else would be the height of foolishness."

"Oh yes, of course. I don't know what I was thinking." Lucy crossed to her typewriter, winding in a new sheet of paper with an efficient air as if to make amends for her stupidity.

Vilho heard Christina go downstairs to talk to Fraser and Timmins. He felt on edge, unsettled. He stared at the blueprints for a conservatory extension to a country house, and wondered why he wasn't losing himself in his work as he usually did.

He realised there was still a deep anger in him at Paul stealing his designs and presenting them as his own work for his own benefit. Until that issue was dealt with, he was disinclined to work on anything else that could be appropriated.

The answer, then, was to concentrate his energy on a project that would hold no appeal for Paul or his moneyed friends. The workers' apartment block, for instance, commissioned by Edward Carter for his factory employees. Vilho and Christina had already threshed out a lot of ideas on the arrangements of the flats, the external design, but what of the rooms themselves? It was the sort of challenge he enjoyed, fitting the necessities of life into a harmonious space. These apartments in particular needed to combine form with function from the outset, there would be no room to expand. Vilho tapped his temple sharply with his fingers. He'd had this very conversation recently. With who?

Ah yes, with Miss Lucy Brown, who as well as being a typist was an energetic dancer with a gregarious group of friends, was passionate about people, and was very clearly nobody's fool. He already knew she lived in a compact flat. She'd mentioned Mrs Corrigan renting the ground floor of a terraced house and Misses Hodge and Smith sharing a couple of rooms. Miss Reed, he knew, had first floor lodgings somewhere nearby. All the experience of self-contained living in a small space was right here in the building. With a broad smile, Vilho picked up his sketch book and went downstairs to the typists' room.

"Ladies, I apologise for disturbing you, but I find myself in something of a quandary."

They all looked up enquiringly. Vilho addressed Miss Reed, momentarily startled, in this new clarity of mind, to find that she had aged from a gauche young woman who had been the youngest in the office to the formidable oldest one who was the backbone of the company. "Miss Reed, we are such old friends I know I can appeal to you as one who has always had the best interests of the firm at heart."

"Certainly Mr Koivisto, what can I do for you?" She reached for a fresh sheet of typewriter paper as she spoke.

"I do not require clerical expertise, but your collective experience. We have the chance of a commission for workers' apartment blocks. There may be opportunities in other places where the client has factories, but only if we get this block correct. Tell me, all of you, what it is that is most necessary in a small apartment? What makes life more pleasant? I can make the rooms comfortable, that is not a problem, but what small or large thing is *needed?* What is so often ignored by landlords who carve up spaces to give themselves profits at the cost of the tenants?"

"A kitchen with storage and space to cook," said Lucy Brown.

"Or even just a tap," said Mrs Corrigan, surprisingly. "So many places don't have their own sinks. It makes all the difference when you have a family."

"A bathroom for each apartment?" speculated Miss Hodge, her bright face interested. "Is that the sort of thing you mean, Mr Koivisto? Smithy and I share one with the other rooms on our floor and all the next floor down people as well, and we have to listen out the whole time for it being empty. It's a terrible nuisance on a Saturday when everyone wants to go out. And when it is free, the water isn't ever properly hot."

"Well-lit stairwells," contributed Miss Reed, entering into the spirit of the discussion. "Natural light during the day and shallower steps for elderly folk. Mother used to find it very trying, God rest her soul."

"Thick walls, so you don't have to worry about babies crying and waking up the family next door," said Mrs Corrigan.

Miss Hodge was still thinking about bathrooms. "Somewhere to hang clothes to dry indoors."

"This is all very useful," said Vilho, writing busily. "I am looked after by the couple who live downstairs in my house, so I have no experience of the practicalities of apartment living. Do please continue."

"A way of keeping food cool would be useful." said Mrs Corrigan. "Even a marble shelf in a stone larder helps."

Miss Reed nodded in agreement. "I have a small icebox. It makes a great difference, but I do have to be in on a Saturday morning when the ice-man does his rounds so I can refill it."

"The last place I worked held a refrigerator manufacturing symposium," said Lucy. "They were saying in ten years' time every family would have a refrigerator of their own."

There was a brief awed silence.

"That sounds lovely, but where would you put it?" asked Miss Hodge.

"It would be worth squashing other things together for food not to go off," said Mrs Corrigan devoutly.

Build in space for the future, wrote Vilho on his list and was suddenly struck by another vista of ideas.

"Storage," said Miss Reed. "There is never space for books and gramophone records where you can easily reach them."

"Not just storage," said Miss Hodge. "Rooms with enough space to fit furniture in. It's nice to have a chair and a table as well as a bed."

"Oh, look at the time," said Lucy, scrambling up. "I should be making the tea. Will you excuse me?"

Vilho got to his feet. "You have all been very helpful. I may intrude another time." He smiled around and left, impatient to commit his half-formed ideas to paper.

Lucy was waiting for him. "I hope you don't mind

my asking," she said, "but when Mrs Corrigan said about making space for a refrigerator, you suddenly seemed to sizzle. I wondered what you were thinking? Did she give you an idea?"

Vilho was so caught up in his vision, it didn't occur to him that this was an odd question for a typist to be asking. After dancing with her at the Black Cat club he thought of her as a pleasant young friend. "You are observant. The situation is that I have a pet project everyone tells me is a pipe-dream. Modular houses, where you start by building three rooms say, then add more when you can afford them, or as your family grows. I suddenly saw I could expand that idea by building *into* the structure as well as on to it. I could include the possibility of adding a multipurpose space and dismantling the internal wall to make a bigger room out of two standard ones."

"In brick?" she said doubtfully. "Knock down walls? Wouldn't the top floor fall down?"

Vilho laughed. "The ceilings would be braced. And not bricks, I would build in wood."

"Wood?" She looked even more doubtful.

"I come from Finland, Miss Brown. My country is seventy percent wood." He beamed at her and ran upstairs to turn his crowding ideas into strong black lines upon a page.

CHAPTER ELEVEN

Jack had intended dropping into one of his clubs after lunch, but a visit to his flat to collect his post altered his plans. Amongst the usual invitations, rambling missives from relatives and answers to advertisement queries, was a letter of more immediate interest. In plain terms, it invited him to come to the Black Cat club at his earliest convenience to discuss the sale of a horse. It was signed 'Rose Milcombe'.

The silken orange foyer wore a distinctly raffish air in the afternoon light. The pulse of jazz from downstairs was absent but the sound of feet thudding rhythmically on a wooden floor, interspersed with sharp instructions, suggested a dance practice was in progress. Someone in the passage beyond the foyer was arguing on the telephone. Jack skirted a cleaner who was leisurely emptying ashtrays into a bin and tapped on the box office window where a catarrhal youth sat reading a fourpenny shocker.

"I've an appointment with Miss Garden," he said. "My name is Sinclair."

The young man didn't look up from the page. "She's rehearsing," he said, as if that settled the matter.

"She sent me a letter requesting this meeting," replied Jack politely.

The denizen of the booth unfolded himself, a sense of injury at having to do some actual work evident in every line of his body. "Wait here," he said ungraciously and stomped down the stairs.

Jack did not wait there. He followed the sound of the telephone call and just managed to hear Youssif Arama say, "I have already assured you the arrangement is to continue and the money will be paid," before his ears detected the youth returning.

"She's coming." And with that the boy slumped back in the booth with Sexton Blake, leaving Jack to await Miss Rose Garden's far more poised and elegant entrance.

There was a flash of recognition in her eyes as she shook hands. Then she led him down the passage to an office with dance scores piled on a cabinet, gramophone records in a case and a framed photograph on the wall of Rose dancing with the Prince of Wales.

Jack hid his surprise. This was clearly her own office, indicating Rose was more important to the Black Cat club than simply the leader of its resident dance troupe.

"I was never so shocked in my life as when I heard the news about Milcombe," he said, languidly disposing himself on a hard chair in front of her table. "I was only talking to him on Saturday night. Chaffing him, you know, about not dancing more when it was such a topping band. It doesn't seem possible."

"It has been a great shock," agreed the woman, pushing aside a small stack of correspondence that Jack itched to explore.

For a sorrowing widow, Rose had herself well in hand. She was dressed in unrelieved black, presumably to establish her bereavement credentials should the police drop in. On most women, this would be unflattering. On Rose, it brought to mind a Belgian lady Jack had encountered during the war whose calling in life appeared

117

to be relieving Bosch officers of both their money and their repressions without breaking sweat.

"It's very good of you to see me under the circumstances," he said.

She inclined her head. "Life goes on, Mr Sinclair. Lamentation does not put food on the table. My husband's apartment is occupied by the police, barring my entry and making it impossible for me to begin the task of settling his affairs, but his valet took the message from Mr Brown where the horse is stabled and had the intelligence to pass it on to me. He was hoping for a tip, of course, or at least for me to keep him on for a week while he looks for another position."

"Daresay he'll find somewhere. People are always changing their valets. Bit of a facer for him though, waving his master off for an evening of amusement, then not having him come home," said Jack. "Still coming to terms with it myself, as a matter of fact. When I first heard, I thought the deal with the horse would be off. Thought I might have to trek up to Milcombe's family's place in Hertfordshire, which would have been an awful bore. I had no idea he was married. When I got your letter, I wondered if he'd made the horse over to you for some reason. Could have knocked me down with a feather when I read your signature. He never puffed it about that he was married at all."

"Nor do I," she said, not offering an explanation. "I prefer to use my professional name of Rose Garden for day-to-day business. The bank is happy with both names." She shot him an appraising look. "Either way, as my husband's sole legatee, I can sell you the horse. Naturally I'd rather the sale took place sooner than later, before the solicitors complicate matters and demand their fee."

"Oh yes, rather. Beastly creatures, solicitors. Mr Brown thought two hundred guineas was a fair price." He looked at her anxiously.

She nodded. "That was the message I received. I'm agreeable, Mr Sinclair, but I have to admit to my share of curiosity. How did you know the horse was for sale?"

Jack had been expecting this. "My fiancée's people are in Newmarket so we regularly see Milcombe at the races. She took a shine to the mare and I said I'd buy it as a wedding present if the price was right. Put the idea to Milcombe, man to man, and we closed there and then."

"He agreed?" Rose's tone was sharp.

Jack gave her a surprised look. "Lord, yes. He has never been sentimental about his horses. Flotsam's only ever had a couple of small wins, you know. He said there was a promising colt he wanted to buy, so he'd use the money for that."

Rose's face hardened. "He would. I suggested selling a horse for... for something else, and he wouldn't hear of it."

Jack let himself show alarm. "I hope there's nothing wrong with the mare? He said she was sound. Maybe I should ask the vet to..."

Instantly, the redhead was all smiles. "There's no need for that. I may not have shared my husband's passion for racing, Mr Sinclair, but I do know he never owned a poor horse in his life. I was surprised he hadn't told me he was considering letting it go, that's all. Would you be agreeable for me to write out a bill of sale now? The manager here and one of the dancers can witness it. They are having a short rehearsal break."

"Oh yes, rather. It doesn't do to let things drag on for no reason, does it? Talking of the dancers, your Kitten Kaboodle are top notch. Even before I saw them for myself I'd heard them mentioned in all sorts of places. Is it only here you perform? Not tempted by one of the theatres?"

"I find the atmosphere at a club more congenial. It is far nicer to be the top attraction than just one turn, lost amongst a dozen others on the nightly bill."

"You've certainly got a good orchestra to dance to. My friends were no end impressed. They've got a lot of gramophone records by them."

"A high-class band was one of the things I insisted on," said Rose absently as she wrote. "That and the floor. You can't have the best club in Soho without them."

It could have been professional sales patter, but Jack detected a possessive note in her voice. She'd had a say in the Black Cat club. Was this her price for lending her inheritance to Basil Milcombe for his Guildford hell?

"Tell me," she said. "When you saw my husband at Newmarket recently, did he win anything?"

"Oh yes, one of his horses came first in one of the big races. Lovely chestnut. I wouldn't be able to afford that one, that's for sure." He gave a laugh.

Her lips tightened again. Her pen moved briefly to a notepad. The note was easy to read, even upside-down. *Where are winnings?*

"Are you nearly done?" he asked. "As soon as it's signed, I'll toddle off to the bank. You've got the name of the mare, yes? Flotsam, currently at Mr Douglas Brown's stud, Newmarket."

"I assure you the document will be quite in order," she said, signing her name neatly.

Jack cast his eye over the contract, not nearly as carelessly as he made out, noting that the lady had astutely slipped in the phrase 'in her present condition', which she presumably considered would cover her if the animal passed away, but which Jack rather thought could usefully stretch to include the unborn foal. He signed with a flourish, turned smartly the wrong way out of the office and found himself in a chilly side passage containing a welter of coats, galoshes and umbrellas. Ahead of him an iron staircase wound its way upwards, to one side was a reinforced metal street door, the other held a padded door. A quick peek through this one revealed a second staircase leading down to the concealed side entrance in the club room itself. In the gloom under the stairs were two bicycles, several collapsed tables and a double stack of chairs.

"Oops," said Jack aloud and retraced his steps to the foyer where the Sexton Blake aficionado was still deeply engrossed. "I'll be back shortly," Jack called. The youth gave no sign of having heard. Outside, the cleaner was smoking a roll-up and bantering with a few of the dancers. Jack nodded cheerfully to him, engaged Enid in a spot of light conversation on the score of having danced with her on Saturday, and continued with his errand.

He considered Rose on the way to the bank. Apart from her status at the club, he hadn't really got very much more than his uncle already knew. Perhaps once she had the roll of banknotes in her hand she would be more forthcoming. He might try a jolly query as to how she and Milcombe had met, or the interests they had in common.

On his return he walked straight across the foyer and down the short passage to Rose's office. She was at the desk, writing, and didn't hear him. He was able to draw close enough to read the words ...*circumstances have changed. We are happy to adhere to your views on not providing female companionship. It is discontinued as from today. May we arrange a meeting to discuss a delay to the...* before she realised he was present and swiftly covered the letter with a sheet of blotting paper.

"That was fast," she said.

"No point letting the grass grow under my feet." He smiled confidingly at her. "Needed to get a move on, to be honest. I'm supposed to be meeting people for cards. They'll be wondering where I am."

"I see." She began to count the notes with professional dexterity.

"At least you won't worry about being robbed of that lot with police on the premises," he said.

Her hands jerked. "Police?"

"Providing they let you into your apartment in the first place, of course." He laughed at his own joke.

She resumed tallying the notes. "Oh, you are referring to Mr Milcombe's flat. I don't reside there, Mr Sinclair. I have my own set of rooms here. Ours was an amicable marriage, but neither of us believed in living in the other's pockets."

"Right." Jack nodded in a confused manner. "Very modern."

There was a piercing squeal from downstairs. "My ankle!" wailed a voice.

Rose stood up, her lips tightening. "Now what," she muttered under her breath, and went to investigate. She was back a few minutes later. "Silly child tripped. No harm done, certainly no need to make such a fuss. Young dancers nowadays don't have the self-discipline I had to learn."

Jack sympathised, made his farewells and walked away with the certificate of sale in his pocket. In his head however, courtesy of sixpence invested with Enid to provide a distraction, was the intriguing nugget of knowledge that Rose had been writing to Mr Forrest regretting their previous differences and asking him to reconsider his decision to sell out.

She thought of the Black Cat club as hers, Jack was positive about that. He could quite see she didn't want to lose it. With Milcombe's death, his shares would come to her, giving her more leverage in how things were run. Evidently she was willing to compromise in order to keep it that way. It begged the question of what other lengths she might go to in her determination to hang on to the club?

He would have liked to bring his uncle up to date straight away, but as he'd told Rose he was due at a session of cards, he headed for the Bath Club. Jack believed in living his cover as thoroughly as possible. He hadn't forgotten there were ruthless people involved in the heroin trade. If they were having him followed, it was as well to give them no reason to doubt his story.

Hubert was kicking his heels in the coffee room and quite willing to oblige with a game of whist. "I'm waiting for my godmother. Said I'd buy her tea in the ladies' lounge. Mother's idea, not mine. I'm only doing it to stop her making a fuss at the wedding. She's never forgiven me for not popping the question to her niece."

Jack cast his mind over Hubert's many connections. "Irene? I thought she'd snagged herself a diamond miner."

"She did. Dripping with the things, last time I saw her. Makes no difference that I did Irene a favour by not offering for her."

"Unaccountable creatures, godmothers," said Jack. He dealt the cards. "Must make conversation difficult."

Hubert shrugged. "She makes pronouncements and I agree with them. I say, wasn't it shocking news about Milcombe? We were still at the club when the police arrived. Topping band they've got there."

"Jolly good, aren't they? The police contacted me too. Got my address from the visitors' book. What did they ask you?"

"Same as they did you, I expect. Did anyone see him go? Was anyone was with him? None of us could help them. It doesn't surprise me he was squiffy enough to fall under a bus. He was there before we arrived, and they were going through the cocktails like fun." He won a trick with a naive look of pleasure.

Jack frowned at his hand and drew a card from the pile. "Milcombe could hold his drink though."

"Pity he couldn't hold his tongue. Did you hear him murdering all those songs? The only time he stopped was when he was up at the bar jawing to a couple of chaps. Pity he didn't talk to them for longer."

"Everyone sings along, Hubert. You do it yourself."

"I have got a better voice. How did you win that trick?"

"By not being distracted." He totted up the scores. "That's a shilling you owe me."

"That's a rotten wheeze, taking advantage of a man when he's down." He paid his losses and looked around gloomily as a boy came in with the message that his guest had arrived. "If I don't survive, tell Amanda I did it all for her."

Lucy was detailed to fetch the tea tray from Mr Kent's room.

"We always clear clients' teas straight away," explained Miss Hodge. "Miss Reed says it looks more professional than leaving the empty crockery on the side for the cleaners."

"Anything that eases through a contract benefits all of us," replied the older woman.

The negotiations in Mr Kent's room appeared to be amicable. When Lucy went in, the older of the two men had just taken a cigarette from the handsome silver box on Mr Kent's table and was about to light it.

"I don't quite see why we couldn't have had - oh," he broke off as his lighter failed. "Wretched man of mine forgot to refill it."

"Allow me," said Mr Kent, reaching into his pocket for a book of matches.

Lucy hid a grin, recognising the distinctive Black Cat motif on the matchbook and remembering her flippant comment to Jack's uncle regarding trade cards.

It was such fun baiting him. She hoped the rest of Jack's relatives had a similar sense of humour. She stacked the tray efficiently and removed it, resigned to not hearing any of the discussion. She'd have to invent what went on when it came to writing her book. She consoled herself by reflecting that while authenticity was desirable, the majority of readers wouldn't have any more idea than she did.

The meeting was still in progress at the end of the working day.

"Not unusual," observed Miss Reed. "Small points being raised, alternatives offered, accommodation reached on both sides. I shall remain until they have finished. They may need notes taking or a witness to a signature."

Lucy slipped the cover on her typewriter reluctantly. Offering to keep Miss Reed company might have been a good excuse to pump her about architectural work, but she was very aware that temporary staff didn't stay a minute beyond their contracted hours. It would look too suspicious. Besides, she needed plenty of time to panic about the art show this evening.

Mrs Corrigan seemed anxious as they walked down the front steps together. "I hope there's nothing wrong. The firm needs this contract."

"Why do you say that?" asked Lucy.

Embarrassment crossed the older woman's face. "I shouldn't repeat it, really, but I overheard Mr Kent say on the phone that he didn't have that sort of money. He sounded most unlike himself. Angry."

"What was it about? Could you tell?" asked Miss Hodge, her eyes round.

"Not really. He said *'That is hardly my fault. I told you I don't have that sort of money.'* Then there was the sound of someone talking at the other end and I think the last words were *'hadn't you'.* Then Mr Kent replied he couldn't because he was dining out with his wife. The other person said something short and Mr Kent slammed the receiver on the stand. I scuttled back into our room quickly. I would hate him to think I was eavesdropping. I wouldn't normally have dreamt of listening, but he sound so angry I couldn't move."

Lucy was intrigued. She had thought since first meeting him that Paul Kent's charm was turned on and off to suit his own purposes. "I wouldn't have been able to either. When was this?"

"On Saturday. Just after I saw your brother. I'd finished typing Miss Kent's report, came out into the hallway to take it up to her and spoke to your brother. He asked for you and I said you'd gone. I was worried he might have been into Mr Kent's room by mistake, but he just thanked me and hurried off, so maybe he hadn't. I hope not. Then I took the report up to Miss Kent who was very nice and asked after Alfred and the children, and when I came down again I heard Mr Kent arguing on the phone. His door was open a little way. He wouldn't bother about that because he wouldn't know there was anyone still here, would he?"

"Golly," said Miss Hodge. "Was Mr Kent arguing with a *client*?"

"That's what it sounded like. I wondered if something had gone wrong with a design and he'd been asked to rebuild for free and was concerned about the cost of the materials."

"It's a pity you didn't hear the whole thing," lamented Miss Hodge. "Then at least we'd know."

"No, only odd phrases like 'it *wasn't enough*' and to '*not to bring her into it*'. That's why I thought it must be about work. I thought he was referring to Miss Kent. Anyway, that's why I was worried about the firm cutting back on staff. I can't afford to lose this job."

"I don't think you need to fret," said Lucy. "Miss Reed didn't seem bothered. I swear she knows more about the company than we do."

Mrs Corrigan's expression lightened. "That's true. Oh well, see you tomorrow."

"Poor thing," said Miss Hodge when they were out of earshot. "Must be rotten for her with an invalid husband and two kiddies."

She prattled on about her friend coming back to their rooms soon, and how she was going to her mum's for tea today for a bit of company, and how she might go to the greyhound track at White City with her dad tonight.

"I've never been," said Lucy. "Is it different to horse racing? It must add to the excitement, being able to see the whole track."

Miss Hodge told her in great detail what it was like. With one part of her mind, Lucy memorised the chatter for if she ever wanted to set a scene at a greyhound race. With the rest, she was worrying about just what her brother had been doing returning to Fitzroy Square after they'd had lunch, when he'd told her he was going straight to his lodgings to study. She'd even seen him in the evening and he hadn't mentioned it.

Her head was so full by the time she reached her flat, she almost didn't know what to do first. She rapidly scribbled 'Aidan' followed by 'greyhounds' in her notebook as a reminder, then set herself to capture the spark of excitement she had sensed in Mr Koivisto when he'd been asking them about apartments. It was a good thing he'd been so intent on his idea that he hadn't queried her interest. He wasn't to know this was the enthusiasm she'd been craving, the zeal she'd been hoping to find. She thought it must be akin to the blazing sense of rightness she occasionally got when she was writing a book and all the motivations and plots suddenly straightened themselves out in her head.

Once finished, she closed the notebook firmly. It would have been nice to get a solid few hours work done on her latest manuscript this evening instead of going out again. She did love Jack but there was no doubt his social activities were eating into her writing time. There was also the alarming prospect of meeting an unknown quantity of his relatives at the show. Rather despairingly, Lucy went to stare at the evening-wear end of her wardrobe.

CHAPTER TWELVE

A little over an hour later, Lucy was so caught up in Jack's account of his meeting with Rose at the Black Cat club that she almost forgot her nerves. That changed as the taxi came to a halt and he piloted her into a brightly-lit foyer, full of people she didn't know.

"Coat on or off?" she asked, to hide her sudden panic.

"Off sadly, otherwise it looks as if we've only called in on our way to somewhere else."

She nodded and headed for the ladies' cloakroom. Inside, a wave of assorted fragrances made her eyes water. She pitied the attendant who took her coat. Fancy having to put up with this all evening.

As she straightened her frock in front of the mirror, wondering if the frivolous rope of green beads had been a mistake, she took herself to task. Why was she so worried about not knowing anyone? She spent much of her working life walking into places where she didn't know anyone. It had never made her feel uncomfortable before.

Behind her, the cloakroom door opened letting in a rich hum of well-bred conversation. That was why. It mattered because these were Jack's people and she loved him and she didn't want anyone to feel sorry for him becoming engaged to a nobody. As if to underline this, two women pushed in next to her to pat their hair and scrutinise their appearance, completely ignoring her.

"Not wearing your new hat?" asked one, taking a slim enamelled powder compact out of her handbag.

"Why, no. My husband said it made me look like a hag so I returned it. Mireille wasn't best pleased, but I told her it was her own fault for selling me something that didn't suit me and I'd thank her not to send in a bill."

"My dear, how intrepid. The last time I annoyed Mireille, she had my spring outfit sewn too tight to make it look as though I'd put on weight."

Her friend shrugged. "Let her try that and I'll take my custom elsewhere. It's only five days across the Atlantic to Saks in New York. I believe I am still a person of consequence there and so I shall tell her."

Lucy thought wryly that her engagement was certainly giving her an insight into how the wealthy spent their time. It would all come in useful. She moved away unnoticed as another friend joined them. "There you are, darling! We missed you at the Claremonts' dinner at the weekend."

In the mirror, a faint wash of colour appeared beneath the American woman's flawless complexion. "My husband was feeling under the weather so we cried off. An early night did the trick. He was fine to take the girls out on Sunday. Come and tell me which of these paintings I ought to admire."

They left in a rustle of expensive tailoring. Lucy looked fatalistically at her drop-waisted green artificial silk with the gold chain belt and reminded herself there were other artists exhibiting as well as Jack's cousin. Hopefully those women belonged to them and weren't amongst his relatives.

He was waiting when she emerged. "You look divine. Don't worry so much. The only person who is going to eat you will be me later on when we're alone."

Warmed by the understanding in his eyes, she collected an exhibition catalogue so Phoebe would get the names right in her 'Society Snippets' article and moved towards the main room. Two steps over the threshold she stopped. "Jack, where exactly are we?"

"At the Wentworth Gallery for Bridget's... oh, I see what you mean."

The clever lighting from the slim columns might have been rose and lemon rather than cerise and turquoise, and the ceiling was cloudy cream rather than smoky grey, but there was no possible doubt in Lucy's mind that the design of this room was a twin to that of the Black Cat club. "I now know why Mr Koivisto was so angry on Saturday evening," she said.

"Two rooms, but with a single idea," murmured Jack. "Which is the copy?"

"This is the original," said Lucy positively. "He asked if I'd ever been to the Wentworth Gallery, then brushed the question off. I can check tomorrow. All I'll have to do is mention I visited an art show here and Miss Reed will give me chapter and verse on when the practice designed it."

"I could also ask Bridget. The reason she was given space in the show is that she works here part time. Meanwhile, brace yourself. Family ahoy."

The crowd parted to show a stately woman alarmingly clothed in a boned velvet evening dress with a matching plum-coloured turban.

"Lucy, let me make you known to my aunt, Mrs Frederick Sinclair. Aunt, this is my fiancée, Lucy Brown."

Lucy summoned up a smile. "I'm very pleased to meet you."

Ignoring her outstretched hand, the older woman barked, "Other one" and inspected Lucy's engagement ring. "Passable. Not lost your eye for a nice piece, nephew."

"I'm glad you agree, Aunt," said Jack urbanely. "I'm of the opinion that my judgement has never been better."

As they moved off towards the paintings, Lucy looked sideways at him. "If that was your idea of starting me off gently, we may need to have a discussion."

He drew her arm inside his. "She is the widow of my father's eldest brother and is under the impression that she rules the family. After her, everyone else will be a piece of cake. Here are Bridget's paintings. I quite like them, but she won't be offended if you don't."

Lovely, vivid splashes of colour met Lucy's eye. "Oh, but I *do* like them. Is that somewhere on the continent?"

He studied the canvas in front of them. "Cap Ferrat, I think. Some of the family were there last summer. Here comes my mother. She will be so gratified to see me doing my duty that she'll put my presence down to you and will love you on the instant."

As a woman dressed in this season's Jeanne Lanvin shantung silk came towards them with a slightly wary expression on her face, Lucy was reminded all over again that Jack's family inhabited a different world. Continental holidays, jewel enthusiasts, haute couture aficionados. How was she ever to fit in?

Her fingers tightened on Jack's arm, but he had spoken no less than the truth. It was impossible not to like his mother, first because there was a family resemblance to Chief Inspector Curtis, and second because of her tolerant amusement at the rest of the family.

"I already know we are going to get on," said Mrs Sinclair. "Bob told me you are exactly right for Jack, which is the greatest relief to a mother's mind."

"That's very kind of him," said Lucy. "I like him too."

"Also you are from Newmarket which is very intelligent of you. Whenever people ask me where Jack's money comes from, I can now pretend he wins it on horses rather than inventing yet more obscure relatives to die and leave him useful bequests."

Lucy grinned. "My mother tells her friends that secretarial wages in London are unfeasibly high rather than admit to them I write detective novels."

"But they are very good! I ordered *Death on the Catwalk* as soon as Jack wrote to tell me about you, and was quite carried away."

There was no time for more as Lucy was plunged into an eddy of small talk with what seemed like some fifty further relatives, most of whom she forgot immediately. The exception was Jack's cousin Bridget, a cheerful, brightly-hued damsel who was immensely entertained by the number of relatives who had shown up to support her.

"Thanks awfully, coz," she said to Jack. "Half this lot wouldn't be here if they hadn't wanted to get a sight of Lucy. Don't let on to the gallery, there's a lamb. They're so tremendously bucked by my popularity that I might even get a second show here. Such a joke when the only reason I got this chance was because the main attraction threw a fit of temperament and didn't send as many canvases as he'd promised."

"There's a lot to be said for being reliable," said Lucy, thinking of her career-girl-adventure publishers who would buy anything she submitted as long as there was a moral every other page and she sent books at regular six-monthly intervals.

"It's a fine space," said Jack. "Who did the design?"

"Before my time," replied Bridget. "The lights can be changed to different filters, but we thought this combination was the nicest."

"It's charming," agreed Jack. "We will now walk all the way around remarking loudly that none of the other paintings are nearly as good as yours."

Bridget clapped her hands over a howl of laughter and sped off.

"You say that," murmured Lucy as they began circulating, "but actually I really do prefer them. Have we met all your people yet?"

"Enough," replied Jack. "Once around the gallery and then we can slip away."

"Lovely to have met you," said his mother when they arrived back at her. "I daresay we'll see each other at several family events now."

"Is that a hint you'd like me to turn up to some of them?" asked Jack.

His mother simply smiled. "You must make him bring you down for a weekend," she said to Lucy.

"All in good time. I don't want to scare her off. Where's Bridget?"

"Over by that ghastly modern stuff. The artist is apparently an *enfant terrible*. Infantile, I call it. At least with Bridget's pictures you can tell what they are supposed to be."

Drawing near Jack's cousin to say goodbye, Lucy saw the women who had monopolised the cloakroom mirror earlier.

"...interesting, but I don't think the men missed anything by not being here."

"Mine will still be at his club. I rely on the porters putting him in a cab at the end of the evenings these days."

"Tiresome for you. Mine is at a client dinner. I'm still thinking about this painting. It's got something, don't you think? I may come back later in the week."

"The name guarantees it will always be a talking point, darling, but have you got a room that can take that much blue?"

Lucy grinned to herself and followed Jack out.

Another day. Jack woke in his bachelor flat thinking it wasn't a patch on waking up next to Lucy. He really must put some serious consideration into when they would be married and where they might live. And also, he realised, as the bedroom door opened and Vickers came in with tea, what he should do about his man. Originally a footman at home, Vickers had, in a *fait accompli* hatched up between his mother and Uncle Bob, accompanied Jack as a matter of course when he took possession of his own apartment.

"I've been thinking about marriage, Vickers," he said experimentally.

"A very sound idea, if I may say so. I have had concerns about Miss Lucy's laundry service for some time. It will be a pleasure to assume control of it."

Well, that answered that. "We, er, rather like Edgar Mansions where her current flat is."

"A suitable address for a newly-married couple. Close to many amenities. I will enquire of the agents whether there are any larger apartments available. I assume she will wish to keep the small fifth floor room as Miss Sugar's darkroom?"

Jack gave up the unequal struggle. "Yes. Thank you, Vickers."

All the same, marriage brought with it other responsibilities. He had never liked relying on his uncle's undercover-operations fund to pay for his lifestyle. That would be scaled down to a certain extent. Travel and a gambling allowance he would still need if he was tracking the sort of clever villains who made money out of other people's misery, but he was determined to provide for his domestic arrangements himself.

With that in mind, he set off for Belgravia to further unravel Mr Trelawny's suspect-dividends scheme. The newspaper payment for the exposé would make a nice addition to the married-life fund.

After tapping on the Consolidated Coca door and receiving no answer, Jack tried the handle and found it locked. He retreated into his own office, waited for a pair of giggling typists to go past towards the kitchenette, then deployed his lock-picking skills.

Everything was as he'd left it, Mrs Antrobus's note lay unread on the desk. Jack began to entertain the suspicion that Trelawny had skipped the country with his ill-gotten gains, except he would surely have checked his post for any extra treasury notes first.

One thing Jack could do, and that was to note down the addresses of the men who had sent the latest requests for unit shares. He locked the door, checked the window would open if he needed to make a quick exit, then rapidly flicked through the card index drawers. Only to draw a blank. Unless they had been misfiled, neither Mr Stone nor Mr Diamond were there. He went through the desk drawers again. He found cheque books marked for each of the four quarters and a spare, presumably for when one of them ran out. Mrs Antrobus had been working her way through the fourth quarter payments and had left a note of where she had got to, but there was nothing else.

He cast a wary eye at the door, wondering if he dare investigate the side desk where the bank book had been secreted. It was a forlorn hope, but Trelawny might have left something personal there that he hadn't noticed at the weekend. His home address, for example, which would save Jack digging for it. Even as he reached for the tray of crockery, voices came from the corridor. The two giggling typists and a deeper man's voice. Quick as thought, Jack opened the casement, climbed sure-footed on to the sill, pushed the window gently closed and inched his way along to his own office.

Emerging with his suit brushed down and a pleasantly vacant look on his face, he sauntered out to the passage. The voice had not belonged to Trelawny. The gentleman in question was sitting in the end office having a robust exchange with someone on the end of the telephone. As Jack passed, the door was kicked shut.

No joy there, then. He walked thoughtfully to the general post office to check on the mail box arrangements. The lockers were in a room off the main post office, sketchily guarded by an official who seemed keener on chatting to customers than preventing miscreants breaking in. Jack looked along the grid of boxes, opened his own and extracted Lucy's dummy letter. He fixed the position of the Consolidated Cocoa box in his memory. It shouldn't be too difficult to stage a distraction in the main room in order to discover what box forty-seven had to offer.

Exiting the room, he paused to fish a tobacco pouch out of his pocket. Jack rarely smoked, but filling a pipe and trying to get it to light was a source of endless opportunity. "Tell me, what's the earliest I can call in to empty my box?" he said conversationally to the official while he tamped down a pinch of tobacco.

"This section is open at half past six, sir."

Jack looked at him, startled. "Good lord, that must be a bore for you. Are there many people here that early?"

"You'd be surprised at the number of regulars. I daresay there must be a good dozen calling in between then and eight, if not more. By five-and-twenty to nine it gets busier still. People collecting their post on the way to opening up their offices, see."

Mr Trelawny amongst them, potentially. "Oh yes, jolly convenient as far as I'm concerned. It must be a rotten job for you, though, standing here day in day out."

"It's not so bad, sir," replied the man with an indulgent smile. "Always someone to talk to, like yourself if I may say so."

"Must get thirsty," objected Jack. "I couldn't do without my tea break."

"Bless you, I get ten minutes for a cuppa when the tellers make theirs, and I'm relieved at lunch time when the afternoon chap takes over. Thank you, sir."

Mornings were out, then. Jack ambled away, mentally restructuring the rest of his day.

CHAPTER THIRTEEN

Christina came down the stairs on Tuesday morning determined to talk to Paul about his appropriating company designs and using them for private purposes. The door of the typists' room was open and she heard Miss Reed say, "Good news, ladies, the contract was signed yesterday."

She smiled. Dear Miss Reed, she was as much a part of the firm as any of them. Christina didn't think it was possible to have a more loyal employee.

"Oh, I am glad," she heard Mrs Corrigan reply.

"I hope you didn't have to wait too long before you could get away?" That was the new typist, the bright one who was interested in everything.

"Thank you, Miss Brown, but it was nothing. The meeting finished twenty minutes after you all left. I was able to complete quite a lot of filing. It's Mr Kent I pity. Not only was he in with the clients all afternoon, he evidently dined with them too. He has already telephoned this morning to say he won't be arriving until his ten o'clock appointment because he is feeling a trifle indisposed. He remarked they must have harder heads than him."

Christina drew in her breath sharply. She had suspected her brother was avoiding her yesterday, now she was sure.

He was one of those rare people who wasn't affected by excess alcohol, so the excuse was a nonsense. He knew she'd been to Radlett for the weekend and that Papa would have mentioned his request to release capital. This was his way of dodging questions. She returned upstairs and asked Vilho if he had a moment.

In her room, she brought him swiftly up to date.

Vilho nodded. "I agree. It is an old trick of his, to look busy and always be somewhere else. No matter, he cannot avoid us for ever. What was the result of the meeting with Fraser and Timmins? What else do they want us to do for no extra money?"

"Not too much. I have it here," Christina passed him a file. "I did look in yesterday, but you'd gone." And she had been unreasonably put out by that and had consequently spent a scratchy evening with her own thoughts and then slept badly. She would walk it off at lunchtime. The family had always been amused at her taking a midday walk whatever the weather. They had no idea it had been a private declaration of independence, the only time she felt she was mistress of her own actions. These days she continued the habit for exercise. Vilho often accompanied her. She always felt better for it.

He smiled. "Forgive me. I had a profitable discussion with our typists yesterday afternoon on the subject of apartment living and was so full of ideas I needed to go home to think them through properly. Wait..." He crossed to his own office and came back with a sheaf of paper. "Here, let me show you my revised drawings for the Carter Industries workers' apartments."

He sat down at the large table and spread the plans out, becoming so enthusiastic that Christina grew as immersed in the project as he was, forgetting for the moment her grievance with her brother.

It had been obvious to Lucy from the moment Miss Reed stopped talking that Miss Hodge was suppressing considerable indignation. She wasn't in the least surprised when the younger woman followed her into the kitchen to offer a hand with the morning tea trays.

She burst out with it straight away. "I couldn't say it in front of Miss Reed, but that was a whopper Mr Kent told about dining with yesterday's clients."

Considering that the leading light of a company didn't have to make excuses to the typists for what time he arrived, Lucy had assumed he had been fishing for sympathy. "Really?" she said, putting the kettle on to boil. "How do you know?"

"Because I saw him at White City," said Miss Hodge triumphantly. "I told you I was going there with Dad last night. Oh, and I had a winner. Two shillings for next weekend's dance. One of Dad's apprentices came to tea and the track too," she added in an offhand voice.

"Oh yes? Does he like dancing?"

Miss Hodge blushed. "He said he might come along."

Lucy chuckled. "Are you sure it was Mr Kent you saw? It doesn't seem much like him."

"Of course I am. He was standing just where he did last time, leaning on the rail watching the racing. It's funny how he wears a different coat to the greyhound track. It's quite fancy, but it isn't his usual style."

"Maybe it's warmer than his town overcoat. I know how chilly it gets watching horses. I expect White City is the same. Did Mr Kent back any winners?"

The younger girl looked puzzled. "I didn't see him lay any bets. He was mostly just talking to various people who came up to the rail to watch and then went away again."

Interesting. "Perhaps he wants to buy a greyhound. There must be more profit to be made in winning than in betting. That could be what the conversation was about that Mrs Corrigan overheard." Lucy was assembling the tea trays as she spoke.

"Golly, that would be a blow to Miss Reed, wouldn't it? She doesn't approve of betting." Miss Hodge warmed the teapots, then watched as Lucy added the tea. "I won't tell her. It would only upset her."

Lucy nodded. "Best not. There you are. You take our tray in. I'll do the rest."

Upstairs, she checked on the threshold of Miss Kent's room as she saw Mr Koivisto also working at the large table. "Oh, I'm sorry, I'll fetch yours, sir."

She did so, carrying both cups across to the table. She caught her breath.

Miss Kent glanced up enquiringly.

"I'm sorry, I saw the words Carter Industries on your drawings and I was startled. I didn't mean to pry."

"Does the name mean something to you?"

Several times over. "Mr Carter is the tobacco millionaire, isn't he? He owned the hotel I was working in over the summer. I didn't realise he was the factory owner you were talking about yesterday, Mr Koivisto."

"And I had no idea he owned a hotel. Is it a modern one?"

"Yes, it's the Bay Sands Hotel at Kingsthorpe on the Lincolnshire coast. It's not been open long but it seemed to be very popular." A sudden idea occurred to her. "Oh! I wonder if Mr Carter might be interested in your modular houses? The hotel was such a radical design that they might appeal to him. The staff were all saying he was planning to develop the area."

Mr Koivisto transferred his attention to Miss Kent who drummed her fingers on the table meditatively.

"The Bay Sands won an award this year," she murmured. And to Lucy, "What did you think of it?"

Lucy considered her answer. "It was striking to look at,

just like an ocean liner. The public spaces were luxuriant and comfortable, the bedrooms were spacious, but the staff quarters were horribly cramped."

Vilho cast up his eyes. "Owners think of their takings, not the practicalities."

"Was there anything else of note?" asked Miss Kent.

"Lots of flat roofing," said Lucy. "The suites with roof terraces were a tremendous draw with the guests, but even at the back of the hotel, the levels were stepped. One of the Russian staff was prophesying problems come winter."

To her secret delight, both architects looked thoughtful, then began to discuss in a measured way how flat roofing was perfectly safe as long as the load had been calculated and gutter runoffs allowed for and other technical terms Lucy didn't follow. She withdrew meekly, leaving them to continue drawing diagrams for each other. Maybe architectural features could spark passions in her new book after all. She only wished she could get on with writing it all down.

After a few minutes, Vilho put his pencil down. "What is it?" he asked quietly.

Christina's hand stilled. *Say it.* "You discussed your modular housing with Miss Brown?"

He shrugged. "Briefly. What of it? It arose out of the questions I was asking the typists about their experiences with apartment living. I am surprised it made such an impression on her that she suggested mentioning it to Carter." He paused, his expression growing incredulous. "Christina, you are not jealous?"

Misery came out of nowhere. Shame. She gave an unhappy laugh. "I don't know, Vilho. I have no right to be. Why should you not discuss your ideas with others?" *But it was his pet project, the one she had thought only she appreciated.*

She stopped and started again. "It was unexpected. And... Miss Brown is vivacious and very attractive, especially in her orange dress. You did tell me you had danced with her..."

Vilho looked at her for a long moment, then crossed to the door, turned the key in the lock against interruptions and came back. "Christina, you are the only woman I will ever love. You know you have had my heart for years. Lucy Brown is an intelligent oddity, far too young for me and very much in love with her fiancé. They are delightful together. I do, however, appreciate your being jealous. It gives me hope that you may yet say yes."

His gaze was steadfast. His eyes were loving and generous and transparently honest. She felt herself tremble. If he had been touching her she would have given way. It came to her that not taking her hand was deliberate. He would always give her the space she needed.

She moistened suddenly dry lips. "I am very close, Vilho."

"Then say it. Will you marry me, Christina?"

To be loved. To be appreciated. To share every hour with him. To combine their hopes and dreams. Never again to have all the responsibility, all the weight of the company and the family on her shoulders alone.

She smiled, not quite believing the glorious joy flooding into her soul. She was going to do it. After all these years she was going to do it. The tide was rushing in and she couldn't have stopped it if she'd tried. She didn't try.

"Yes," she said.

After a very long interval, during which the touch of his lips on hers and the feeling of his arms around her sent her into such a vortex of elation that the rest of the world ceased to exist, she sat on the bench seat next to him marvelling that after so long she had given in between one heartbeat and the next.

He held her hand loosely. She thought perhaps his heart, like hers, was too full for words. Then he spoke.

"We will see Paul together this afternoon."

On his way to Scotland Yard to catch up with Chief Inspector Curtis's investigation into the Black Cat club and Milcombe's death, Jack regretted he couldn't ask his uncle for police help in tracing Trelawny. He'd have to make do with his wits and his newspaper contacts until he had proof of wrongdoing. Not that it would stop him casually mentioning his progress on the story.

"Unless you've got more information to add to the note you sent me first thing this morning, you can go away," said Curtis. "I'm busy."

"I thought you might appreciate a fresh pair of eyes on the evidence."

"There is no evidence. We've interviewed everyone who was still at that benighted club at midnight and all we've got for it is pouches under our eyes. Poor old Maynard had to show his wife his warrant card before she recognised him."

Inspector Maynard, working at the desk in the corner surrounded by bank books, quarterly résumés and a mighty stack of bills, chuckled at this sally.

"No drugs even?" asked Jack. "I saw one of your chaps pretending to be a cleaner yesterday."

Curtis gave a reluctant grin. "Not a shred, crumb or stray corner of packaging has he found. Mind you, they haven't promoted him to cleaning the offices yet. As regards Milcombe, we've identified several people who left at the same time, but none of them noticed him particularly. One interesting point *has* arisen. Rose Garden has no alibi. She left the bar area shortly before midnight. Enid Bursall thought she'd gone upstairs, but the dancers who were changing said they hadn't seen her and she wasn't in the dressing room. Daisy Brickett had a feeling she'd nipped out into the alley for a change of air, but she can't pin down why she thinks that. She and Enid left with Aidan Brown and went in the opposite direction to Milcombe." He looked at Jack blandly.

"I had much the same thought," said Jack. "Rose wants control of that club. She could have left via the side exit and walked part of the way with Basil. Just a normal, everyday marital chat away from prying ears. They seemed amicable enough earlier, so he wouldn't have been expecting a push."

"Would she have been strong enough?" mused Maynard. "The post mortem report indicated bruising consistent with a forceful push on the upper back."

"She's a dancer," replied Jack. "A very good one. Dancers have strong muscles and fast reflexes. One of your eye witness reports mentioned a woman, didn't they?"

Curtis made a disparaging noise. "They mentioned everything bar a talking horse."

"What does the lady herself say?"

"That she was in her office and saw no one."

Jack made a face. "Which could equally be true. All the offices are out of sight of the foyer. Did you find anything useful at Milcombe's flat?"

His uncle smiled. "Oh yes. A very nice haul. A quantity of heroin wraps, loose cash and an overflowing bureau, the contents of which are currently driving Maynard to an early grave. Care to cast your eye over it? See if you can spot anything out of character for a man of society."

Jack needed no second bidding. He seated himself at the end of Maynard's table and familiarised himself with the various piles of paperwork. "I see he subscribed to the school of thought that you don't pay a bill until it's been presented half-a-dozen times."

"Unless it was to do with his horses. Those were all paid promptly."

Jack nodded. "That fits. Did he keep a cash account?"

"If you can call it that," said Maynard. "In the red ledger. He wasn't what you might call the most diligent of scribes."

For the most part, it was as Jack had expected. Payments to Lucy's father and brothers for training fees, foaling care and veterinary bills. Racing prize money paid in. Covering fees paid in. Sale fees of non racing stock paid in. There were all the normal outgoings, quarterly rent on his service flat, membership of London clubs, reluctantly-paid bills. Where possible, he had paid by cash to avoid the tuppence on cheques. So far so ordinary. A picture of a gentleman on the fringes of society treading a fragile line between success and insolvency. More cash drawn out than his expenses would indicate necessary, and a great deal of cash paid in at irregular intervals without any hint of where it had come from. The last payments into the account had been made a week before his death.

"It looks to me," said Jack after a while, "as though the cash paid in falls into two camps. There are small irregular payments of up to fifty pounds a time - those trickle in and cash trickles out - and then there are whacking great lumps arriving shortly before he makes a large purchase. I wonder if... no, that can't be it."

"What can't be what?" asked his uncle.

"I was thinking dividends, but these sums aren't quarterly."

"There are no dividends," said Maynard. "All his declared income came from his horses."

Jack did a swift calculation. "I can see why he'd be constantly on the lookout for more. No mention of the Black Cat club? The dancers we were talking to thought he had money in it and from the tone of Rose's conversation, it was clear she at least has a management stake."

"Oh yes, didn't I say?" said Curtis, looking across.

"That's one thing we have managed to establish. Basil Milcombe has a large shareholding, as does our friend Mr Forrest. The document is with the solicitor. Forrest put up the finance to get the club going, taking shares as security. Milcombe was very gradually paying him back and buying him out at the same time. That's where the profits will be going."

Jack ran his eye along the monthly totals. "Rapid cessation of payments into the account coinciding with his Guildford hell being closed down. Jump forward a few months and everything picks up again. At a guess, that's when he discovered how much money there is to be made pushing drugs."

"That's our thinking."

"There are still those large cash payments in. Did he indulge in a spot of blackmail? That would be enough to drive some poor sap to murder."

"The team combing his rooms have been looking for anything incriminating. So far there's no sign of a safe or handy loose floorboards for a cache. The grieving widow, incidentally, has demanded an itemised list of everything we take out of the flat along with where it was found."

"She knows there's more there."

"She suspects there is *something* there. However, there are any number of anonymous keys on his ring, so he could have safety deposits the length and breadth of England for all we know."

"Tracking them down will be an amusing job for somebody," said Jack. He got to his feet, frowning at the books. "There's something on the edge of my mind and I can't fish it out. Anything you'd like me to do?"

"Cut back on your visits to the Black Cat club. With Milcombe's proven involvement, we've got enough for a search warrant, but he didn't have rooms or an office there and it's the drugs gang I really want to catch. We're keeping it under observation in case there is another dope delivery. Arama and Miss Garden are being tailed for external assignations. It all depends how far into Milcombe's confidence they were."

"Can you trace calls? There was the snatch of conversation I heard with Arama saying everything would continue as before."

"That came from a call box. It shows they are on edge, which is when mistakes happen. I'd rather you weren't there complicating matters. Run away and follow your normal routine."

At this no-so-subtle hint, Jack left, the two tickets he'd already bought for the club's gala evening on Wednesday burning a hole in his pocket.

CHAPTER FOURTEEN

Lucy managed to rattle down some hasty notes about architectural design under cover of typing up a very boring, very detailed quote. She was hopeful of squeezing in a bit more when she went for lunch. The difficulty was her tendency, when writing in her notebook in the café, to lose track of time. She frequently had to tip the waitress to warn her when it was ten minutes to the hour.

Today, Miss Reed had returned from her own break and was preparing to cover for the receptionist who had gone to lunch a few minutes before.

There was a clatter of high heels in the hallway. Miss Reed hurried out and Lucy heard her say, "Mrs Kent, how pleasant to see you. Do please take a seat. I'll find out whether Mr Kent has finished with his client yet. I'm afraid I've only just got back from lunch so I don't know what..." The soothing platitudes broke off with a sudden cry.

A cool American voice that was oddly familiar said, "Oh my, how clumsy of me. Make sure to give my husband the cleaning bill."

As Lucy reached the doorway she found Miss Reed gazing with horror at the front of her skirt which was marred by a large splash of ink. An opened ink bottle lay on its side on the floor in a spreading puddle of permanent blue. It was clear what had happened. The absent receptionist had been careless in replacing the lid and the visitor, not noticing, had put her handbag down on the desk, knocking the bottle off.

Lucy resourcefully pulled two sheets of blotting paper out of the pad and gave them to Miss Reed. "One each side of the material and press together. I'll get a cloth." She dashed to the kitchen and came back with several, casting one down straight away to soak up the ink. Fortunately the flooring was an extension of the Victorian tiling in the hallway rather than the modern fashion for parquetry. The visitor retreated delicately to a chair.

"Leave that," said Miss Reed. "Check whether Mr Kent is still busy with this morning's client, and let him know his wife is here."

Always putting the company first, even when her nice skirt was dripping with ink. Lucy crossed the hall, tapping on Mr Kent's door before going in.

He was on the telephone with his back towards her. "Nothing of the sort. It's true I was originally repaying a loan, but that's finished." He swung around and saw Lucy. "I have to go. I can't help you further. Yes?" he asked as he replaced the handset in the cradle.

"Mrs Kent is here, sir."

His face went blank for the briefest moment, then he strode to the door, smoothing his hair. "Marion! How delightful. Now don't tell me I was due to join you for lunch and I've forgotten?"

Lucy slipped out of the room behind him. Under cover of mopping up the ink, she peeped sideways at Mrs Kent and realised why she had sounded familiar. She was the American woman who had been at the gallery last night. Her mission today was to bear her husband off to view the outsize blue painting and persuade him what a focal point it would make for their dining room.

The front door was just shutting behind them when Miss Kent came down the stairs. "Ah," she said. "I wanted a word with my brother, but I appear to have missed him. Goodness, whatever has happened here?"

"An accident with a bottle of ink," said Miss Reed. "Nothing to worry about."

"Your skirt would beg to differ," observed Miss Kent. "You had better go home and put it in to soak at once. I am sure Miss Hodge can fill in on reception." She returned upstairs, shaking her head slightly at Mr Koivisto who was waiting at the turn of the flight.

"You really should," Lucy urged. "We've blotted the worst of the ink, but it does need seeing to. It's not as if you live far away and the firm owes you an extra half hour for staying late yesterday."

Miss Reed gave an irritated sigh and put on her hat and coat again. She was followed out of the door by Miss Kent and Mr Koivisto, talking together in low voices.

"Mind the phone while I go to the lav, there's a duck," said Miss Hodge, flying down the passage.

Lucy bent to finish wiping up the ink just as the phone trilled. Typical, she thought, wrapping a cloth around her hand to protect the receiver. "Paul Kent Architects, may I help you?"

"Put me through to Paul Kent," said a woman's voice.

"I'm afraid he is at lunch. May I take a message?"

"He can't be," said the woman sharply. "I was only just talking to him."

"He left a few moments ago with his wife."

"Did he indeed! Well, you can tell him..."

There was a crackling noise. In the background, a man said, "Rose, we need to speak about the arrangements for..." Then the sound went dead, as if the caller had put her hand over the mouthpiece.

"I'm sorry, there must be a fault on the line," said Lucy. "I didn't catch that. Could you repeat it please?"

"Tell him I'll be in touch," snapped the woman and rang off.

"Look at your hands all inky," said Miss Hodge, bustling back and installing herself happily behind the reception desk. She cast a covetous glance at the picture papers provided for waiting clients.

Lucy nearly replied that she was used to it, but stopped in time. "I thought I might as well clean up the ink on the floor properly once I'd started. I've got some good strong soap at home for myself. Thank goodness for gloves, eh? No one will notice."

"And you've missed most of lunch," said Miss Hodge.

"There's still time for a bun if I'm quick."

"I bet Mr and Mrs Kent won't be having buns. Did you know she used to be an heiress and a Society Catch before she married Mr Kent. Mum said she was so beautiful that when the engagement was announced, one of her suitors threw himself off Westminster Bridge in despair. What was she wearing today?"

Lucy almost laughed aloud at the perfect opportunity to fish for information. "A sable coat and a teal brocade dress with a wide black belt. It was very striking. She does have lovely clothes. She was in a burgundy satin evening gown yesterday at the art show my fiancé took me to. It was at the Wentworth Gallery. His cousin had some paintings in the show."

To her gratification, an animated look came over the other girl's face. "Ooh, Mr Koivisto did the designs for the Wentworth Gallery. I remember typing it all up. Smithy and I went to see what it looked like once it when it was finished. It was ever so interesting, finding out what the plans and all the lists of materials had turned into. We don't get the chance when it's people's houses, but a gallery is public, isn't it? It looked luscious, all crisp and clean."

So that was that confirmed. But what did it mean?

Jack had been reading a newspaper on a bench outside the Belgravia post office since midday. With his head bent and his hat pulled low over his brow, he was able to keep a perfectly adequate watch through the open doorway at the comings and goings. Partly this was to familiarise himself with how the change of security guard by the mail-box room was managed and partly because if Trelawny had a legitimate job that took up his working day, he might take advantage of his lunch break to nip across town to collect his post. Not that it would help without a description to go on, but Jack was confident of his ability to recognise the face of any gentlemen he saw now if they showed up somewhere else in his vicinity.

He turned a page of the newspaper leisurely as the post office official of this morning was relieved by another chap. Jack gave it another few minutes, then strolled inside and took his time about checking his mail box. At the doorway, he repeated the performance with his pipe and asked when the latest was that he could access his box.

"Seven o'clock, sir, but if you're expecting something urgent, you can go around the back to the sorting office door and ask them to let you in. They work through the night. It depends who's in charge as to whether they open up for you."

"Oh, I wouldn't do that. It seems an awful cheek. Are there many who do?"

"A handful, sir, no more than that. It's not a regular disturbance."

"Seven o'clock will do me. I wouldn't want to spend my evening worrying about post." He gave the man a friendly nod and left.

Making notes at the desk with his door partly ajar, he remembered the newspaper advertisement that he himself had replied to. He checked today's *Courier* and there it was again. *Small outlay, guaranteed returns.* It was too much to hope Trelawny had given his home address when he paid for the insertion, but there was just a chance the classified-ads clerk could provide a description.

Thinking of payments, Jack wondered if he could get a line on the unit shares people missing from Trelawny's filing system by asking Uncle Bob about tracing the numbers on the banknotes he'd found in the envelopes. One of them had been new. It should at least be possible to track it to the issuing bank, if not any further. He copied them all down anyway and addressed the note to his uncle at the Yard.

Jack glanced at his wristwatch. Half-past two in the afternoon felt like the perfect time for a spot of larceny. Unfortunately, half-past two was also when the third floor got lively. The gentleman at the end, who never seemed to talk when he could shout, tramped past with a cup and saucer in his hand, the giggling typists settled down for a gossip by the head of the stairs and the letting agent arrived to show a client one of the other empty offices. Jack locked up and headed for Fleet Street.

The grizzled counter clerk at the classified-ads desk of the *Courier* was an old acquaintance and quite happy to chat. This may have been because he was under the impression Jack worked for the police. It may equally have had something to do with the tip Jack invariably left him.

"Every three months regular. Trelawny is the gentleman's name. Pays in cash for a daily repeat."

"What does he look like?"

The clerk scratched his head. "Bluff sort of chap. Good clothes. Middle aged. Stouter than you, sir, not as tall. Favours a dark homburg and tan gloves. He's been coming in for two or three years now."

None of which left Jack much wiser. As a matter of form, he asked about the other suspicious adverts he had noticed. One had been placed by a financial broker that

Jimmy Ward had already mentioned as having the worst judgement in the City. One was a bankrupt businessman under a new name. One was unknown.

"Always someone who wants to make money without working for it, isn't there?" said the clerk. "Daft to fall for it though. Not that you can blame them with wages being cut and prices going up."

Jack slipped him a tip and left sombrely. Wages down, prices up and still the privileged set spent money carelessly on their own amusement.

He put this unpalatable fact to Lucy in her flat that evening.

"True," she said, "but at least the Lester twins' money, to take an example, benefits the dressmakers and milliners and silk stocking manufacturers who clothe them. Their quest for amusement helps towards an income for the waiters and chefs who serve them, for the dance bands whose records they buy."

At her matter-of-fact words, Jack's world slipped back into place. "Bless you. I've been spending too long with bad-news stories. You are right, of course." He became aware that Lucy wasn't her usual ebullient self. "So that's me set to rights. What about you? What's wrong?"

She looked at him, her eyes troubled. "There's something going on at work to do with Mr Kent. I know I'm only there for the research, but I can't help being involved."

Jack gave her a swift kiss. "Lucy Brown's besetting sin. She cares. What sort of something?"

"There was a muddle at lunchtime and I had to answer the phone. It was a woman for Mr Kent. I said he'd gone to lunch which was true because his wife came for him. Oh, it turns out she was the American woman at the gallery yesterday, the one who liked that gigantic blue painting."

"Just shows money can't buy taste."

"It doesn't buy manners either. She knocked a bottle of ink over Miss Reed's skirt and didn't even say sorry. Isn't that mean? And yet Miss Hodge reckons one disappointed suitor threw himself into the Thames when she accepted Mr Kent."

"I found that story in the archives," said Jack drily. "It actually happened significantly *before* the engagement was announced."

Lucy tutted. "It's shocking, the way reporters manipulate facts to get a good story. Anyway, to get back to what I was telling you, the woman on the phone got very sharp and said she'd only just been talking to Mr Kent. Then she said she'd ring back and slammed the phone down."

Jack raised his eyebrows. "Chickens coming home to roost, eh? We did think the other night he was a ladies' man."

She nodded. "It's not that. It's that I interrupted a call just before Mr Kent went to lunch and he was saying he'd already paid back the loan. Then he said he couldn't help any further and rang off."

"So?"

"I didn't recognise the woman's voice in my call, but in the background someone was shouting for Rose. It would be quite a coincidence for Mr Kent to know two people called Rose, wouldn't it? There was that packet of drugs in the booth of the Black Cat club where he was sitting, remember?"

Jack looked at her in consternation. "I'd almost forgotten that."

"The thing is, Aidan was earning a little money running errands for Basil Milcombe. After he left me on Saturday he went back to Fitzroy Square. I only know because Mrs Corrigan met him in the hallway. Putting it all together, I can't help wondering if Aidan was there to deliver a replacement package to Mr Kent, not to see me at all."

"If Kent is using drugs supplied by Milcombe, he'll never tell."

Lucy shook her head. "I don't think he's an addict. I think he is supplying them to other people. He told Miss Reed he had been out with clients on Monday night, but Miss Hodge saw him at the White City greyhound track. He wasn't betting, just watching and talking to various people who came up to him for a few minutes before leaving again."

Jack winced. "I'll ask Uncle Bob to have him shadowed. I'm afraid it could be messy for your firm."

"Miss Kent does most of the work anyway." Lucy paused, then added reluctantly, "Mr Curtis should talk to Aidan again. Ask who else Basil paid him to deliver to. I'd quite like to see Aidan myself, come to that."

"Where will he be now?" asked Jack.

"What day is it? Tuesday? It's his Anatomy day. They do revolting things with dissection and drawing muscles and looking at bones and joints. It goes on quite late. I daresay he'll be back at the Black Cat club tomorrow though, ready to defend Daisy's honour at a moment's notice."

Jack sighed. *Sorry, Uncle Bob.* "You'd better rustle up some glad rags for their gala evening, then. We will go and prove we're only there for the company and the dancing."

She nodded, her face lightening, and returned to her typewriter. Jack pulled the prints of the Consolidated Cocoa bank book towards him but found himself getting muddled between these entries and those of Basil Milcombe's this morning.

"I'm losing my touch," he muttered. "What are you looking so pleased about?"

"I'm putting your trick with the desk into this book. I was going to tape the villain's incriminating document to the underside of a drawer, but hiding it against the wall is much more elegant. Who says crime doesn't pay?"

With a jolt, Jack realised he hadn't checked underneath the furniture in the Consolidated Cocoa office. He was so shocked at his lapse that he said it out loud.

Lucy favoured him with an old-fashioned look. "Even for Miss Reed's investments I'm not going out again tonight. Besides, what might there be?"

"Trelawny's post office box key?"

She shook her head decidedly. "Too inconvenient. He'd have to come in, release the key, get the mail and tape it in place again. Why would he bother?"

Jack sighed in gloomy assent. "I should have checked it all more thoroughly. Let me think. Tomorrow is the last day Trelawny can leave Mrs Antrobus's pay and instructions before she comes in again. If the office still looks like the Marie Celeste, damned if I don't do a little light burglary. I might also stage a small distraction at the post office and see if I can't get inside box forty-seven."

"How are you going to do that? I can't help, I'll be at work."

"Ask no questions and I'll tell you no lies. I have my methods."

"Show off," she muttered and returned to her typewriter.

CHAPTER FIFTEEN

Wednesday morning - and while the rest of the building was full of the buzz and clatter of office life, the Consolidated Cocoa office did indeed appear unvisited and unloved. Jack was fairly sure by now that Trelawny had a legitimate job elsewhere. Even so, he locked the door and secured his window escape route before making a proper, thorough search of every piece of furniture in the room.

All to no avail. There was nothing more. Leaving the office as he'd found it, he walked down the road to the general post office, idly flicking a sixpence in the air and catching it as he went.

Ten minutes later, during the indescribable pandemonium caused by a street urchin losing control of his dog amongst the queues of people awaiting their turn at the counter, he had opened box forty-seven, grabbed a large handful of letters from the top of the pile, closed the box again and thrust the envelopes into his own open box. Then he strolled to the doorway, congratulated the red-faced official on successfully chasing the mongrel and its boy off the premises, strolled back to empty his box and returned to his office to investigate the booty.

There was no money this time, but amongst the

enquiries to the adverts were two letters of note. One said the ten pounds for Mr Ruby's units had been given to the messenger. The second contained the information that twenty pounds had been paid to the bearer and Mr A Gate would like to extend his commitment at the earliest convenience.

Jack leaned back in his chair and whistled. He had no need to check the records to know neither Ruby nor Gate appeared in the card index of Consolidated Cocoa clients. Just what was going on?

"I understand Paul is unavailable again today," commented Vilho. "Is he avoiding us on purpose?"

Christina smiled a little ruefully. "Why would he when he doesn't know we have discovered his secret? His diary says he is drumming up custom in Ealing."

A tap at the door heralded Lucy with the post. A burst of noise from the ground floor followed her. A strident female voice, raised in anger.

"Is there some disturbance?" asked Christina.

"A lady is asking quite vehemently for Mr Kent."

"He is out of town today."

"She says she doesn't believe us." She glanced at Vilho. "I know who she is, Rose Garden from the Black Cat club. She is the leader of the dance troupe. I think she wants to see Mr Kent on a personal matter."

"Then he is definitely out of town," said Christina drily.

Lucy took a quick breath. "My fiancé's uncle is Curtis of the Yard. He is very interested in the Black Cat club. If you could see your way to finding out what the lady wants, it could be useful."

Christina awarded the younger woman a thoughtful look. "You are full of surprises. I *could* talk to her, though I daresay my brother would not thank me for it."

"I too would like to know more about that club," said Vilho, "notably, the circumstances under which they obtained the designs." He met her eyes blandly.

"Very well," said Christina with resignation and went down to where a striking red-head was confronting the receptionist. "I'm afraid Mr Kent is visiting clients. If you would like to tell me what it is about, I will see he gets the message."

As she opened her brother's door to usher the visitor in, Lucy Brown flitted down the stairs and returned to the typists' office. Christina made a mental note to talk to that young lady very soon.

"It's Mr Kent I want to see," replied the woman. "Mr Paul Kent."

"He will not be in until tomorrow. I should have introduced myself. I am Miss Kent, a partner in the practice. May I know your name?"

"Partner, eh?" The visitor looked at her appraisingly. "Maybe you *can* help me. Professionally, my name is Rose Garden. Privately I'm Mrs Milcombe."

Christina kept the polite look on her face. The Milcombes were a Hertfordshire family. The practice had advised them on some alterations a few years ago. "I see. Is Mr Kent working on a project for you?"

"Not any more. He did the designs for my nightclub in part-repayment for a loan my husband made him. I'm here to ask for the rest of the money." She studied the room appraisingly. "It shouldn't be too difficult. He can sell a couple of these paintings for a start."

So that was it. What a fool Paul was. Living above his income again. "That would be a personal matter, not a company one. You have the loan agreement?"

A flicker of annoyance crossed the smooth face. "It was informal. A gentlemen's arrangement. I do know there is still a thousand guineas to pay back."

"I am not doubting you," said Christina. "The difficulty is that without an official document, signed by both parties, there is no proof. Perhaps your husband could..."

"My husband's dead. I can't ask him where he recorded it," snapped Mrs Milcombe. "I need the money now. I have an option to buy the remaining shares in my club. The seller won't give me forever to come up with the cash."

Belatedly, Christina took in her visitor's black outfit. "My commiserations on your loss," she said quietly, "but without proof of the loan, I cannot..."

"Proof? Why else would Paul have done the designs for free?" She stood up angrily. "I hoped, being a businesswoman like myself, you would be reasonable. If you won't, there are other ways." She nodded at the framed photograph on the desk of Paul, Marion and the girls. "His wife wouldn't like to hear some of the stories I could tell. Nor would your fancy clients, I don't suppose. He's got a very free and easy way with him when he's off the leash for the night. Believe me, I know what I'm talking about. Let your fine gentleman know I want my money and I want it now."

She swept out. It took Christina a few seconds to compose herself. The vitriol in the woman's voice had been nasty. Exiting Paul's room, she saw Lucy standing in the doorway of the typists' room, concern in her eyes.

"Shall I make your tea early, Miss Kent? It won't take me long."

Christina looked past her to the open door and pitched her voice a little louder than normal. "Thank you, that's very considerate. Bring your notepad with you. You can take a letter for me while it is still fresh in my mind."

Upstairs Vilho looked up from where he was working at the table. Despite herself, Christina smiled. Vilho had never believed in being idle.

"What was that about?" he asked.

"Paul. Owing money, amongst other things. The lady was unpleasantly insistent on being repaid. It might explain why he has been stealing from us." *This time at least.*

Vilho's mouth twisted in distaste. "Is she one of his liaisons?"

"Without a doubt. Let me gather my thoughts."

He moved across to the bench seat to sit companionably next to her, taking her hand loosely, calming her by his very presence. She felt regret again for all the years she had wasted, and blind fury at Paul for letting his sordid affairs intrude on this magical time of discovery. Vilho only relinquished her hand when Lucy Brown entered, balancing a tray.

Christina felt a sudden revulsion about making their squalid troubles public. "On reflection, you need not have brought your notebook. Mrs Milcombe wanted to see my brother on a private matter. I cannot imagine your fiancé's uncle would be interested."

She received a surprisingly direct look from Lucy's clear green eyes. "Chief Inspector Curtis always says if statements have no bearing on a case, he forgets them, but until he has a complete pattern, he can't tell what is irrelevant. Is it something to do with the designs for the Black Cat club? I, um, was at the Wentworth Gallery on Monday."

"It is inevitable, Christina," murmured Vilho.

And after all, why should she continue to make Paul's life easy when he had never once done the same for her? She shrugged. "Mrs Milcombe says the design was in part-repayment of a loan her husband made to Mr Kent. She wishes for the remainder of the money. Apparently she has a chance to buy more of an interest in her club."

Lucy flipped open her notepad. "If you would like to tell me the conversation, I can type it up and you can sign it. Then I can give it to Mr Curtis and you won't need to be bothered again."

Christina hesitated.

"Talking helps things not to fester," added Lucy apologetically.

Fester. The girl did have a way with words. "Who are you, Lucy Brown?"

"A nice girl with useful connections," said Vilho. "Take it down, Lucy, while I pour the tea. Then, perhaps, we can all get back to work."

Faced with this, Christina gave in and related the interview as near word for word as she could remember. "How extraordinary," she said. "I do feel cleansed. What a dangerous young woman you are. Bring it up when you have typed it and I'll sign."

Alone again, Vilho kissed her softly. "The sooner we have a long talk with Paul, the better. I am not minded to let his peccadillos spill over into our work any more."

Christina nodded. "I agree."

"I also think you should forgo your usual lunchtime walk and instead visit a jewellers with me to choose a ring. Naturally I am prepared fight for you until death, but I feel discussions with both Garth and Paul about the practice will proceed more smoothly with visible proof of our attachment on your finger."

Slipping the two new letters into an inside pocket along with the original ones, Jack locked the rest in his desk and headed back to the Yard. In his uncle's office, Curtis and Maynard were in overcoats and hats.

"Sorry," said Jack. "If you are busy I can come back later."

"You've got five minutes. Messy robbery in the City overnight. Nightwatchman left for dead. What is it?"

"Two things. Aidan Brown was running errands for Milcombe. Lucy thinks he may have unknowingly delivered dope to her boss, Paul Kent. Kent may then have supplied lesser fry at White City on Monday. That is informed speculation, but it would still be worth you asking Aidan who else he delivered stuff to for Milcombe."

"Noted. I'd like your reasoning on the drug speculation."

Jack handed him the notes he'd made. "It's all in there. The other thing is my elusive friend, Trelawny. I'm beginning to think he might be useful to you." He spread the letters on the table. "No addresses. Plain script and envelopes. None of these men are in the files and just look at the names."

Curtis scanned them intently. "You think Trelawny is providing an accommodation address?"

"Something like that. If so, he must be in on the fiddle because there's nothing to distinguish these envelopes from his unit shares ones. One of the banknotes is new. That might be traceable."

The telephone rang. Maynard answered it. "On our way." He looked at Curtis. "The car is ready for us. We can ask Fenn and Draper to fingerprint the letters when we get back. Might turn up some old friends. Those names, though, they're ringing a bell."

Curtis quirked an eyebrow. "Stone, Diamond, Ruby... I agree they sound like code words. Leave it with us, Jack. If you do get a sight of Mr Trelawny, you might try following him. Don't get caught and keep an eye open for other watchers."

Jack nodded. "Always do. I'm not keen to have an accident like Basil Milcombe."

Maynard turned around in the act of opening the door to leave. "Milcombe! That's it." He crossed to the other desk and thumbed hastily through a small notebook. "There, what do you think of that? This was in Milcombe's bedside drawer."

Jack looked at the spread pages. It appeared to be a list of jewellery. He read it aloud. "Two loose stones, three diamonds, two agates, four emeralds, one ruby..." He met his uncle's eyes. "These have to be connected, surely. The amounts coincide with the multiples of ten pounds in those letters. Do I remember you saying he had a number of unknown keys on his bunch?"

"They're in Milcombe's box of effects. We have to go, Jack."

"And lo," said Jack, selecting one and bringing forth his own Post Office box key. "Number forty-seven, as I live and breathe. Also the key to the Consolidated Cocoa office. It seems I have been keeping observation on a dead man. Shall I fetch the contents of the mail box for you? Word of honour I won't open them this time."

"It would save us the trouble," pointed out Maynard.

"There are more letters in the office. I can take both keys and bring you those too?"

His uncle nodded. "Put them all in a large envelope. Seal it with date and time. Ask the clerk to leave it on my desk if we're not here. This could be an all-day job."

Jack followed them down to the street and watched as they climbed into a car that already held his old friends Sergeants Fenn and Draper. He got out his own notebook and wrote down what he remembered from the list. There had been colours as well as jewels used as code words, and letters next to each name. BC, WC, D...

He returned to his flat for envelopes, thinking deeply.

Vickers materialised as he was about to go out again. "I have ventured to make you an appointment for tomorrow evening to view a first floor apartment in Edgar Mansions, sir. It is rather larger than Miss Lucy's present set of rooms and seemed very suitable to me. The tenants are expecting to give up the lease shortly before Christmas. I have asked the agents to hold it, pending your approval."

Jack looked at his man blankly. Sometimes he wondered why Vickers went through the rigmarole of asking for his opinion. "Thank you. I'll tell Lucy. Your own department was suitable, I take it?"

"Two rooms, usual offices and an adequate pantry, separated from the main accommodation by a baize door. The tenants will be away for a few days from tomorrow. The concierge has instructions to show you around whenever it is convenient."

"Admirable." He refrained from asking Vickers whether he could actually afford the new flat and instead left for Consolidated Cocoa.

True to his word, Jack emptied the contents of box forty-seven into one large envelope, and the post from the Consolidated Cocoa office into another. He sealed both and wrote the date across the flaps.

Then he extracted the bank book from the second desk. Now he knew Trelawny was Milcombe, the pattern of transactions made a lot more sense. Jimmy Ward had been right about the unit shares being working capital. It wasn't for a garage though, it was to fund Basil's racehorses. Thinking back to the meticulous racing accounts, the discrepancies between those and his personal bank account were explained. The injections of cash had come from Consolidated Cocoa. Every money-making scheme Milcombe had undertaken had been to bolster his string of horses. The misery he had inflicted on his victims through gambling, blackmail, financial hardship and now drugs hadn't mattered to him as long as he was able to pursue his main interest.

Was there anything else to learn from the pass book? Initially, Milcombe had only kept sufficient in the account for his investors' quarterly payments. Jack assumed he had kept up with those as he was unwilling to lose a useful source of referrals. Two years ago, however, large cash payments into the account began to appear.

Jack gave a sardonic grin. That would coincide with his marriage. Whatever Rose said about separate establishments, he'd bet there wasn't much about her husband's ostensible income she didn't know. Presumably the Consolidated Cocoa account was a useful place to keep winnings and stud fees away from her acquisitive fingers. She could have no idea his Trelawny alias existed or she would have pressed Milcombe harder for the money to buy out Forrest's share in the Black Cat club.

Jack turned to the final entry in the book. Two thousand pounds had been paid in last Friday. That was the day after the Newmarket meeting when Milcombe had received prize money and had betting success. It brought the total in the account to well over five thousand.

Jack gazed thoughtfully at the drawers of index cards, filled with all the people Milcombe had conned out of their savings. He looked at the bank book again. The original money had been obtained fraudulently. Rose was unaware of it. It was held in the name of a man who didn't exist. This five thousand pounds could be tied up for years while solicitors wrangled over who owned it. And tomorrow was Thursday.

Grim amusement rippled through him. He took the cover off the typewriter and inserted a fresh sheet of paper.

Dear Mrs Antrobus,

Apologies for your wasted journey on Monday. Circumstances beyond my control have necessitated the closing down of Consolidated Cocoa. Starting at the beginning of the index, please make out refund cheques for the full holdings of as many investors as you can get through during your normal hours on Thursday. I will finish the rest myself. I enclose seven shillings in payment and appreciation of your services. Leave the office key with Elljay Associates next door.

He then carefully extracted the cheques that had already been signed by 'Trelawny', signed the note with a passable imitation of the signature, left everything tidy and retired to his own room.

CHAPTER SIXTEEN

"Hello," said Lucy, coming out of Paul Kent, Architects to find her fiancé waiting for her. "This is becoming a nice habit, meeting me for lunch. Are you missing me or is there something you want?"

"Every day is a barren desert without you in it," declaimed Jack with his hand on his heart.

Mrs Corrigan chuckled and trotted away.

"Of course it is," said Lucy. "Never mind, I've only got one more week here, then your days can be filled with as much verdant pasture as you like. I'm glad you are here. I've got information for your uncle."

"I'll trade you. I've got news too. You have no idea how busy I have been this morning."

"Good afternoon, Sinclair," said a voice behind them.

Lucy turned to see Mr Koivisto and Miss Kent shutting the front door and walking down the steps.

"Christina, this is Jack Sinclair, Lucy's fiancé. I met them both at the Black Cat club. Sinclair, Miss Christina Kent. We won't keep you. Miss Kent likes to clear her head with a brisk walk before allowing herself to eat. As I am hungry, I am encouraging her to do so without loss of time." He nodded at them in a friendly fashion and neatly turned Miss Kent in the opposite direction. Lucy saw her tip her head up towards him and say something that made him laugh.

"Are they romantically involved?" asked Jack, watching them.

"Clever, aren't you?" said Lucy. "I think they must be, but they may have only realised very recently. Do you want to hear what I have found out?"

"Yes, please, and then I'll tell you *my* news."

"Rose Garden came in this morning breathing fire and brimstone and asking for Mr Kent. He wasn't in so she saw Miss Kent instead. She says he borrowed a large sum of money from Basil Milcombe some time ago. He designed the Black Cat club in part repayment and now she wants the rest of the loan back. What do you think of that?"

Jack whistled softly. "So that's the link. How do you know? Have you been listening through keyholes?"

"Can't be done without someone asking what you are up to. I told Miss Kent your uncle was Chief Inspector Curtis and that he was interested in the Black Cat. She dictated her statement for me to pass on. I think she was glad to. There was a nasty suggestion at the end that Rose and Mr Kent had been having an affair, which fits with what we saw that first time. It wouldn't surprise me. He certainly trades on his charm."

"But not with you."

"Stop fishing. I prefer the rugged, dangerous type." She got Miss Kent's envelope out of her handbag. "Here you are. Can you give it to your uncle?"

Jack stowed it in an inside pocket. "I'll leave it at the Yard for him. There's been a burglary with violence in the City, so he and his team are busy. *My* news is that our Mr Trelawny is nothing more than an alias for Milcombe."

Lucy stopped. "No. How?"

He tugged her arm to get her moving. "You're causing

an obstruction. He invented himself an alias. Where shall we eat? This looks like a nice café."

She glanced through the window. "It's busy, so it must be good. How infuriating," she added as they made a dive for a corner table and agreed with the waitress that poached eggs on toast with a pot of tea sounded just the ticket. "Your discovery is far more impressive than mine."

"Once I started thinking about it, it made sense. He collected his post Saturday morning, intending to go back on Sunday to sort it out and leave the clerk's pay. But Sunday never arrived. How much did Kent borrow from Milcombe? I'm amazed he let any cash out of his hands."

"I don't know. Rose was aware of the loan, but didn't have written proof. She says a thousand guineas is still outstanding. I don't think she'll get it back from Mr Kent without a receipt. That must be what he was talking about on the telephone conversation Mrs Corrigan overheard."

"She'll take Milcombe's rooms apart looking for the docket. She's already asked Uncle Bob for an itemised list of everything they've removed. He gave her short shrift and asked if she wanted the mystery over her husband's death solved or not."

Lucy chuckled. "I can just see him. He's got a deceptively mild manner. Is he any nearer knowing?"

Jack shook his head. "It could be our old friends the drug barons," he said and told her about the code in the letters. "My feeling is the names Milcombe marked as BC got their dope from the Black Cat club and paid for it there and then. The other consignments were delivered either by himself or by others. The ones who got their supplies from a third party sent the payment to the post office box mentioning their code name, so he could tick them off."

"And if they didn't pay, he'd send the heavies after them."

"Either him or the people further up the chain. They are the ones Uncle Bob really wants."

Lucy met his eyes for a moment, remembering how ruthless those people could be.

"Never mind that," said Jack. "What are we doing tomorrow evening? Vickers has found us a bigger flat and thinks we should look at it before he takes it for us. It's on the first floor in Edgar Mansions. Available in the New Year."

Lucy's fork clattered to the plate. She stared at him, suddenly unable to breathe.

His eyes danced wickedly. "Eat your nice egg. Don't you want to be married? I do."

"I... yes. I just wish you'd give a girl some warning. It's a bit of a leap, going from murders to marriage in two sentences."

"We can talk about the murder again, if you like."

Lucy eyed him. He was enjoying himself enormously. "What I always ask in my detective stories is what sort of person was the victim? What did they care about? That could give a clue to why they were killed."

"Milcombe didn't care about anything."

"Horses. He really cared about his horses."

"I stand corrected. Yes, that's what all his moneymaking was for. I'd hazard a guess the Black Cat club was set up primarily as a venue where it would be easy for clients to get hold of drugs, where the flow of people in and out of the door would be unsuspicious. He would pay for the consignment in cash and give Arama a consideration out of the profits. He hid as much as he could get away with in the Consolidated Cocoa account along with his winnings from racing. He could then show Rose his personal bank account to prove he couldn't afford to buy Forrest's shares. He'd rather the club changed hands than make over any of his precious prize money. That was earmarked for more horses."

"And if the club failed?"

Jack shrugged. "He'd do what he always does and move on to another venture. He wouldn't care."

"But Rose would," said Lucy slowly. "It gives her a pretty hefty motive. With Basil gone, she could sell his horses."

"I agree. She really wants that club in her own hands. It must have infuriated her to know Milcombe had the means to buy out the loan and wouldn't do it."

Vilho was aware of Christina walking alongside him, swerving automatically to avoid passers-by, locked into her own thoughts.

"They make a nice couple," she said. "I see what you mean about devoted."

"They are well-matched, even if they make me feel old. Christina, when did you see Lucy in her orange dress?"

She shot him a sideways look that in any other woman he would describe as shamefaced. "At the weekend. I was so very, very cross about Paul's deception. I was furious and restless. I tried to telephone, then remembered you had said you were going to the Black Cat club. I decided to surprise you. I drove back from Radlett, parked in the side road and walked around the corner. I wasn't... I wasn't thinking very clearly. There were a group of people in front of me, young and high-spirited. I suddenly realised I wasn't dressed for dancing and probably looked a fright anyway. I went into the small restaurant next door for coffee. I sat at a table by the window wondering if I would even have the courage to call to you when you came out of the club. That's when I saw Lucy Brown and Mr Sinclair arrive. She was hanging on to his arm and looked utterly charming. I don't know how long I sat there. I had more coffee and some sort of sweet cake. The waiter was Turkish and I think he thought I needed it. I saw you leave, intent and thoughtful, but by the time I got to the door, you had gone. I lost my nerve, paid and drove back to Radlett. No one knew I had even been away."

"What were you hoping for?"

"I hardly know. I wanted - needed - to see you." Her voice dropped. "If you had asked me to stay, I would have done."

For a moment, the ability to breathe left Vilho's body. "I love you very much, Christina," he said. "Here is the jewellery shop and over the road is the Copper Grill where we can celebrate with steak and fried potatoes."

She smiled up at him. "That sounds suitably decadent."

Vilho smiled back. "After we have chosen the ring I would like to make an announcement to the company, but it would be politic to tell Garth first, yes? In person?"

"I would rather."

"Then we will go today straight after we finish work. Carter is not coming in until Friday. I can afford to take one evening off the design."

She looked at him, her eyes full of humour. "I hope Papa appreciates the sacrifice." Then she added soberly, "It means we can't challenge Paul until tomorrow."

Vilho shrugged. "He may not even return to the office today. We can address both issues at the same time. I refuse to think about Paul when we are about to choose the most beautiful ring in the world for the woman I love."

She rested her hand on his arm. "So be it."

Jack walked Lucy back to work, then dropped into the Bath Club on the way to Scotland Yard, hoping to find Theo or Hubert there. He was in luck. They were both absorbed in the *Racing Post*.

"You survived your godmother then?" he said to Hubert.

Hubert folded his paper. "Brushed through. Are you dropping into the gala evening at the Black Cat tonight? The girls have been practising another routine."

"Rather," replied Jack. "That band's hot stuff. That reminds me. Argument with Lucy. She says Milcombe arrived on Saturday after we did, I say he was there before. What do you think?"

"I don't like to contradict a lady, but he was already there when we arrived and that was earlier than you," said Hubert. "You remember, I told you I felt bad about wishing him at the devil when he was singing along off-key at the next table all evening and talking loud enough to drown out our conversation. If I'd known he was going to do that I'd have asked for a different table before we sat down."

That was one thing that had been niggling Jack. "Don't envy whoever has to sort out his affairs. Didn't you say he had investments?"

"He said he had. Knowing Milcombe, they'll be on the shady side. He offered to put me on to a good thing. Always a rum do in my experience."

"He didn't tell you the name of them?"

"Choked him off. Didn't trust him."

Theo nodded sagely. "Rotten taste in clothes. Never trust a man who wears a blue tie with a red coat."

Jack stood up. "I'll remember that. Got to be off. Did I tell you I've bought Lucy a racehorse? Good notion of yours, that. She's pleased as punch about it. See you later."

He ambled away, leaving them to look after him open-mouthed.

Curtis and Maynard had just returned to the Yard when Jack arrived, but were evidently about to have a conference regarding the City robbery.

"I know, you're too busy to talk," said Jack, forestalling his uncle. "I'll be quick. Here are the contents of the Trelawny mail box. Also a statement from Miss Kent via Lucy saying Milcombe had loaned Kent a large sum and was pressing him for repayment."

"Interesting. Put it with the rest," said Curtis, nodding towards the box with Milcombe's case notes and effects in.

"What time did he get to the Black Cat club, do you know?"

"About eight pm. Why?"

"Lucy thought it was much later, while she was still being Phoebe. She recognised his chequered overcoat."

"He was wearing an evening overcoat when he was brought in," rumbled Maynard. "There was a dark red and grey checked coat in his flat. It's on the inventory."

"Ah," said Jack. "That's the one he wore at Newmarket. I dare say there are a number of them around." He dropped his envelopes in the case-box and idly picked up the inventory.

"Are you thinking about mistaken identity now?" said Curtis quizzically. "Go away, Jack. We are about to be very busy."

"Good luck," said Jack. He sauntered out of the room, made a note of the tailor's name that had been recorded next to the checked coat, and left in the direction of Bond Street.

Lucy, when he met her from work asking if she was ready for an evening of high living and dissipation, was astonished that Milcombe had arrived so early on the previous Saturday.

"But I saw him go in. I could have sworn I recognised him. He was the same build. Same overcoat over his dress suit. He was wearing it at Newmarket, but with a homburg rather than a top hat. You must remember it. I thought how typical it was that he wasn't wearing an evening overcoat."

"Uncle Bob says Milcombe *was* wearing an evening overcoat."

Lucy stared. "How odd. I'm sure the man was familiar."

"The tailor says they've only sold half a dozen of that pattern in the last few weeks. Too bold for their normal clientele. I believe he hoped I might be more discerning."

"You led the poor man on, you mean. Did you get the names of the customers?"

"He assured me they were all country gentlemen, thus I could wear it around town without fear of an embarrassing matching encounter. I doubt it matters, anyway."

"No, but it's going to irritate me, wondering why I thought I knew whoever it was." Her brow wrinkled as they joined the crowd trying to get into the underground station. "He may have been in the background of the last photo I took."

"Can you enlarge it?"

"Yes, but it won't be very clear as I was focusing on the foreground."

An hour later, looking ruefully at an abstract print of a top hat and a checked overcoat, Jack agreed that as a line of enquiry, it had just petered out. "It was worth a try," he said. "Let's change and eat and catch up with your misbegotten brother."

CHAPTER SEVENTEEN

On the way to Radlett, Christina contrasted her state of mind with the last time she had driven this way. "Less than a week ago," she said wonderingly. "I can hardly believe I'm the same person."

In the passenger seat, Vilho laughed and stretched his legs. "When life changes, it changes completely."

"As far as Papa is concerned, it should never change at all. I hope he doesn't fly into one of his rages. Not that he can do anything about it, but it makes for an unpleasant atmosphere and I am sure it does him no good."

"We will tell him gently, but firmly, and stress that our marriage will make no difference to the functioning of the company. Garth is intelligent enough to see when bluster will not avail him."

He was so calm, so assured. Christina felt herself relax. "I should have said yes to you years ago."

"That is in the past," he said tranquilly. "Shall we go to Finland for a holiday next summer? I would like to show you the forests and the lakes where I grew up."

Christina drove and listened as he described his family home and in no time they were at Radlett. The housekeeper exclaimed over her ring and wished them happy. "That'll put a smile on your father's face for sure," she said.

Which just showed you could be in a post for ten years and still not know a thing about your employer.

"Couldn't have come at a better time," continued Mrs Drake. "I haven't said anything yet, but I'll be giving notice shortly and moving to be near my daughter. She needs help with her family and her husband's practice and blood's thicker than water when it comes down to brass tacks, isn't it? I don't like to leave you in the lurch, but it won't matter now you're getting married because you'll be coming back home again."

"We shall be sorry to lose you," murmured Christina, making a mental note that this was something else to see to. "I'd be grateful if you didn't mention it to my father just yet."

"Wait until he's in a better mood, eh? Your news will do that. He'll be overjoyed." She bustled off to the kitchen to acquaint the household.

Garth Kent was not conspicuously overjoyed. "I suppose you'll go your own way as usual," he grumbled. "What does Paul think?"

Vilho's look of surprise was perfectly judged. "Naturally we have told you first. I cannot see Paul objecting since it will not make any difference to the company. The three of us have always worked together in partnership, we will continue to work together."

"Married women didn't go out to work in my day."

Garth's future son-in-law smiled. "I believe it would be easier to stop Christina breathing than to stop her designing. The firm would not have half its present success without her."

"Talking of which," said Christina, "we will need to drive back early tomorrow as we are working on the presentation for Carter Industries. Mr Carter and his associates are coming in on Friday."

Garth scowled. "Modernist, I suppose?"

"Modern, certainly," said Vilho, "but with a handshake to tradition."

"The practice has to move with the times, Papa. Mr Carter's approval of the designs for his workers' apartment blocks could open up more markets for us."

Her father's eyes gleamed at this familiar argument. "Why do you need more markets? New buildings are a risk. We built our reputation with solid, sympathetic conversions."

And had missed out on designing new houses for the suburbs because of Garth's and Paul's prejudices. She wasn't going to miss out on this. "There are fewer country-house families needing conversions just now," she said briskly. "That reminds me, I had a visit from a Mrs Milcombe saying she was a widow. I couldn't place her. I know we did some work for them a while back."

"Milcombe?" barked her father. "We converted one of the coach houses to provide quarters for the estate steward. Paul did it. He was at school with the younger son. Bit of a ne'er do well, that one. Heard a shocking thing about him recently. Crowned a disappointing career by walking under a bus. That'll be the widow you met. Old Milcombe had no idea the son was married. He was in such a temper that the whole county knows by now."

Christina smiled, encouraging Garth into more general conversation. "How did you hear?"

"How do you think? Housekeeper told me. She said Cook heard it from the butcher's boy. Why I pay a pack of women to sit around gossiping all day I don't know."

Christina prudently didn't mention that before long he wouldn't be.

The jazz band was already pumping out syncopated rhythms when Lucy and Jack arrived at the Black Cat club. Jack showed their tickets, nodded in a vague, amiable fashion to Youssif Arama and piloted Lucy down the stairs to the dance floor.

"What makes it a gala night?" she asked, thinking it didn't look that much different to the previous times they'd been here.

"Spot prizes, competitions, novelty dances, first cocktail on the house."

"Competitions?"

"Certainly. Just watch Amanda and Julie Lester out-foxtrot each other for the sake of a two-shilling prize."

Lucy slanted a glance at him. "High life palling on you?"

Just for a moment, his eyes were bleak. "Sometimes. I went into journalism to make a difference, not to watch rich people make idiots of themselves over what could be a week's rent for a poor family."

"That's the penalty of *undercover* journalism. Look, there's Aidan. You can find out who else he delivered Basil's nasty little packages to. Put a couple of dream-sellers out of action."

"Uncle Bob would skin me alive." He brightened up. "Still, what is life without risk? Good evening, brother-in-law-to-be. Have you decided how much you'd like to borrow?"

"Nothing," said Aidan. He turned a radiant face on Lucy. "Daisy says they don't have to go with customers if they don't want to any more so she doesn't need to buy out her contract."

Relief rushed through her. "That's splendid. I'm glad they've seen sense at last. Maybe having the police all over the club at the weekend has brought home how close they were to breaking the law."

"I'm glad whatever the reason. Now I can concentrate on my studies and save for the future instead."

"Qualify, buy into a practice, marry and start a family," said Jack.

Aidan's fists curled. "Is there something wrong with that?"

"Not at all. It sounds perfect."

Was there was a hint of wistfulness in his voice? Lucy took a sip of her drink and put it back on the table. "This is vile. I'm not surprised it's free. Has Mr Curtis asked you about delivering for Basil?"

"He called me out of a lecture to grill me. Thank you so much for ratting."

"Don't be silly. Basil's contacts could be important. Why didn't you tell me that was why you were in Fitzroy Square?" Lucy didn't need Jack's raised brows to know this was a leading question. This was why she always made her fictional detectives amateurs. So much more scope for enquiries than the police. She drank some more of her cocktail with an insouciant air.

Aidan looked embarrassed. "Lucy, I couldn't. You were so pleased to see me, I'd have felt a heel saying I wasn't there to meet you. Then at lunch, I realised how much you disliked Milcombe, so that gave me another reason not to mention it."

"All right, you're forgiven. I can see why you were furious when you realised *he* was the reason you needed to run his errands in the first place in order to build up money for Daisy's buy-out price. Good thing you had an alibi seeing her home."

Aidan winced. "I didn't."

Lucy put her glass down, feeling suddenly sick. "I beg your pardon?"

"I didn't take Daisy home. I was going to, but she told me not to be daft because the conductor would see they were all right and the bus goes right past their hostel and there wasn't another one back, so I'd have to walk. I put her and Enid on to the bus, waved them off and then went back to my digs. No alibi at all."

Lucy gazed at her brother in horror. No alibi and mad as fire at a man who would shortly be pushed in front of a bus? This was a disaster.

Jack signalled the waiter to take their cocktails away and bring glasses of lager instead. "Tell me everything Milcombe said to you in the car on the way back from Newmarket. He was killed because of the sort of person he was. There may have been a clue in his conversation."

"He started by saying what a rum do that tied race was, and that he'd noticed I was upset at not winning more. He said he wasn't going to ask questions, but he could put me in the way of earning a couple of pounds by making a few deliveries for him if I wanted. I said I didn't have much free time and he said this would mostly be at the weekends. He'd already got people to help him out during the week. And that he'd never believed in keeping all his eggs in the same basket. I didn't have a clue what he was talking about. I dozed off when he started talking about shares and dividends. When I woke up again he was worrying about the mare he's got in foal at Doug's place, the pretty one Rick was concerned about. I say, what will happen to her now?"

"Flotsam? Jack's bought her for me."

"That's good. He'd have liked that. He was quite different when he talked about his horses. I almost liked him then. That's partly why I was so mad when I found out it was him who was the part-owner here, as if I'd been tricked."

"People are frequently disappointing," said Jack. "Do you want to dance with your sister while there's still room to move? As soon as the Lester twins arrive there will be elbows and flying feet everywhere."

In other words, we've been sitting here looking serious for too long. "Come on, Aidan," said Lucy, standing up and ignoring the way the room took a moment to steady itself. "You'll need to practise to keep up with Daisy."

More people flocked in while they were on the dance floor. The club certainly looked as though it was going to be busy for its gala night. *Too many people. Too hot. Too noisy.* The coloured lights swam into each other. Lucy was glad of her brother's steadying arm.

"Sorry, Aidan," she said. "I need to sit down."

"Are you all right?" he asked.

"No," she replied. "I don't know what was in the house cocktail, but I don't think it agreed with me. I'll ask Jack to take me home after Daisy's first dance."

"I'm not going to stay either," said Aidan. "I've got studying to do. Now I know Daisy will be all right, I won't need to be here so often. Trust is important, isn't it?"

"It's probably the most important thing there is in a relationship," said Lucy. Her eyes followed Rose Garden as she led her dancers out to the band's usual crashing fanfare. There was a woman who hadn't trusted her husband an inch.

The routine was as stupendous as before. Aidan blew a kiss to Daisy and left. Lucy, after an unpleasant interlude in the ladies' lavatories, was very ready to follow his example.

"Better?" asked Jack, looking for a cab to flag down.

"Much," said Lucy shakily. "It's left me feeling really sleepy though. I wonder what caused it? I'm never ill."

Jack's voice acquired a hard edge. "I might give Uncle Bob a ring. Youssif Arama didn't look nearly as sorry as he should have done that two of his customers were leaving early."

Lucy's stomach threatened to rebel again. "They put something in my drink? You think they may still not be sure of us and want us out of the way just in case?"

"It's not beyond the bounds of possibility. Mine tasted

foul too. Fortunately I only had one sip and I've got a lead-lined stomach. Here's a cab. Can you contrive to lean against my shoulder and groan gently?"

"I won't even need to pretend."

She was vaguely aware of Jack talking urgently on the phone when they got back to her flat, then making her a cup of tea and coaxing her off the sofa and into bed.

"I'll be here if you need me, but it looks to me as if you swallowed something not on the menu before nature took a hand. You'll be all right in the morning. Which is more," he added pensively, "than the person who doctored your drink will be if I ever catch up with them."

"Good news," said Paul, coming in to Christina's room on Thursday morning. "Mrs Ingram has decided what she wants at last. A grand conservatory with a bathing pool and divans set around it. Very Alma-Tadema."

Christina looked up from Vilho's new staircase plans for the Carter Industries building. "You're not seriously suggesting we design it? She'll change her mind again next week. Paul, I wanted to..."

"She's certain this time. We invited her to dinner last night and she was discussing it with Marion. Marion was marvellous, really fired up her enthusiasm for the project. She's coming in at half past nine. I'd like you to join us to discuss time-scales. The sooner we get going on this the better. I've put a lot of effort into it, don't want her going off the boil now." He dashed jauntily down stairs again.

"Paul is in his usual form, I see," said Vilho from the doorway.

"Put in a lot of effort indeed," muttered Christina. "He's put in a lot of *social* effort. He may even have sketched some designs. I don't for a moment imagine he's come up with costings or practical considerations."

"That's what we are for," said Vilho drily. "We will have to leave it until after the meeting to talk to him."

Christina fumed at the waste of time, and fumed even more when Paul announced his intention of whisking Mrs Ingram off to lunch after a meeting in which she had been enthusiastic about every suggestion either of them made without actually committing herself to saying yes.

"We'll get the plans drawn up then," said Paul, ushering his client out to the reception area and helping her into her coat.

That means me. Again. Ready for you to sell on to someone else. Christina was sufficiently nettled to say, "I was hoping for a word today, Paul."

"Certainly. I'll pop up as soon as I get back. I can leave you with these plans, can I?"

She nodded frostily and returned to her room.

One look at his uncle's unforgiving face told Jack exactly why he had been summoned to Scotland Yard this morning.

"Tell me, Jack, what was the difficulty in complying with my instruction to leave the Black Cat club well alone?"

"Lucy needed to see her brother. She was then taken ill, as I informed you last night, but seems fine today. She insisted on going to work. I insisted she take a sandwich for lunch which she will eat on the premises. I'll meet her from there at the end of the day."

"Sense at last. And is she happy, now she knows young Mr Brown does not have an alibi?"

"You knew about that?"

"Jack, I am aware you regard righting wrongs as a quixotic adventure, but we in the department are not amateurs. We interviewed and followed up everyone leaving the club at around the right time. Aidan Brown saw the two young dancers on to the bus - which did indeed deposit them outside their hostel - considered going back to have his grievance out with Milcombe, caught a glimpse of him at the end of the road talking to - he thinks - a woman in a fur wrap, changed his mind and walked off his temper by pounding the pavements homeward."

"A woman? Rose Garden?"

"It's a working hypothesis. One of several. She does own a fur wrap. Daisy Brickett says she was wearing it on Saturday. However, Daisy also says she saw Milcombe's red and grey checked overcoat hanging in the side passage on Saturday night, so I'm not taking her observations as gospel."

Jack frowned. "A lot of the staff use that coat rack. What does Enid say?"

"She can't remember earlier, but says it wasn't there when they left. Which it wouldn't be as Maynard logged it at Milcombe's flat. Now, returning to last night..."

"Did anything happen at the Black Cat club after we left?"

"A visit from one of the couriers we have been keeping tabs on. The gentleman in question suffered a brief, painless assault shortly after leaving the club, but when asked by the bobby who came across him, claimed nothing had been taken. This in itself is odd as the modus operandi at this level is for the courier to receive payment for the consignment before leaving."

"Weren't you following him?"

"I repeat, Jack, we are not amateurs. How do you think the constable on the beat got to him so fast? The thief meanwhile, who makes a habit of these swift extractions, was tracked to a very interesting warehouse which we are even now making plans to raid."

A well organised, choreographed manoeuvre. It pointed to big business. "Ingenious. Courier delivers dope, collects payment, is robbed in a useful alley so if he is stopped and searched can legitimately claim nothing is ever anything to do with him and lives to ferry more drugs another day."

"It's how they work. Layer upon layer of deception. We'll get them eventually."

"And the Black Cat club?"

"Due for a spot check any minute now. Without Milcombe directing the operation, there will still be a lot of incriminating evidence on the premises. I'm grateful for the tip-off, but stay away from now on. That's an order. The person behind Milcombe's death could still be one of the drug barons. Put it about that you've taken a dislike to the place after your young lady became ill."

With a certain irony, Jack borrowed Lucy's words from the night before. "I won't even need to pretend."

CHAPTER EIGHTEEN

"I've sent Mrs Ingram off happy. I think she'll sign as soon as we've done the detailed plans. What did you want to ask me?"

Christina looked at her brother, trying to recall when he had turned from an engaging young man with a ready smile and the world at his feet into this superficial portrayal of a successful businessman. He stood there, a yard into her room, door left ajar emphasising that he could only spare her a few minutes, scented with cigar smoke and flushed with a lunchtime half-bottle of wine.

"It's about the designs you have been stealing from the firm and re-selling on your own account," she said, deliberate and precise. "It's theft, Paul. It's got to stop."

He smiled with the same easy charm that thirty years ago had caused the cook to blame the gardener's boy for her missing rock cakes rather than him. "What are you talking about? That's ridiculous. Why would I do that?"

"Presumably because you are living above your income. As to how I know, I was at Radlett over the weekend. Stella Payne was waxing lyrical about her sister's conservatory which I know did not pass through our books."

"It's hardly uncommon for architects to take on private work."

"The plans were in your chest. They were an exact copy of the ones I did for the Lucases of Westmoor Place. They weren't the only plans in there."

The wine flush had left his face. "You snooped amongst my private papers?"

"No more than you must have done when you stole *my* early designs for your student portfolio."

"What nonsense. You are losing your mind, Christina. I've been worried this might happen. It's a common phenomenon amongst single women of your age."

"Don't bluster, Paul. That was simply an example. I'm talking about *now*. I know why you need the money. The woman from the Black Cat club was here yesterday, saying you still owed the balance of a loan her husband made you. He was pressing for payment which is why you designed the nightclub for free, using Vilho's ideas."

"Complete farrago. Rose was obviously trying to see what she could get out of you. Not quite out of the top drawer, as I expect you realised. Milcombe made a bit of a mistake there, poor fellow." He caught her look of incredulity and hurried on. "It's true I borrowed a small sum from Milcombe when I had a tricky patch with school fees, but that was paid back long ago. It was a misunderstanding on the part of the bank and Milcombe offered to tide me over to save any unpleasantness with the school. That's why I discussed various design ideas with him when he went into the nightclub business, returning the favour, so to speak."

"Paul, you drew the plans for the Durbans' conservatory only this spring. And if the loan to Mr Milcombe had been paid back, why were you at the Black Cat club on Saturday night?"

He extracted his cigarette case from his pocket and flicked it open. "I wasn't. I was at home. I wasn't well and Marion cut the dinner to stay with me."

It was his automatic-denial tone. She knew it of old.

"You were at the Black Cat club," she said wearily. "I saw you. I was there, waiting for Vilho. You walked right past my car. You were wearing your new overcoat, the one Marion doesn't like."

"My coat is hardly exclusive. You saw someone who looked similar to me, no doubt."

"Paul, you're my brother. It was you. I'm not going to argue any more. Renegotiate the wretched loan however you like, but please do it legally. Don't worry, I'm not going to tell Marion anything, but stealing from the firm has to stop. Vilho agrees with me."

He drew a sharp breath, his fingers poised in the act of selecting a cigarette. "You have discussed it with Vilho?"

"Naturally. He is a vital part of this company and you know it."

"I would have thought family loyalty would…"

"The moment I start covering up theft, I'm complicit. And if we are talking about family, Vilho has asked me to marry him. I said yes."

For two, three heartbeats, her brother said nothing at all. Then he smiled. "He's got around to it at last, has he? Well, that puts a different complexion on things. I couldn't be more delighted. We must have a party to celebrate. What are you doing this…"

From self-righteous denial to fulsome congratulations. She didn't think she could cope with much more. Fortunately there was a rattle of cups as Lucy brought the tea tray through the open door. She was accompanied by Vilho himself. Never had Christina been more relieved to see him.

"Christina, Miss Brown has a useful suggestion. Oh, sorry, Paul. I didn't realise you were in here."

"He is just leaving. What is this suggestion?" She took the tea and lifted the cup to her lips gratefully.

"It is regarding the workers' apartments. Miss Brown has invited us both to her flat this evening for a first-hand view of the usual way facilities are crammed into an inadequate space. Having absorbed our ethos here, she believes we could come up with something much better. There is also a larger flat in the same building which she and her fiancé are viewing this evening. It seems an ideal opportunity. I think we should go. It will give us a head start on tomorrow's meeting with Carter."

"How very thoughtful of you to suggest it, Miss Brown," said Christina.

The young woman looked a little as if events had overtaken her. "Miss Reed is always saying how everyone should pull together for the good of the company. Mr Carter has a lot of sites. A successful design could lead to more contracts with him."

Paul struck a match and drew on his cigarette, throwing the spent matchbook into the waste basket. "Do you know Mr Carter?" he said, sounding amused.

Lucy's eyes had followed the arc of the matchbook. Now her gaze snapped back. "No, not at all," she said, looking alarmed. "I've never even met him. I only know how particular he is because I had a job in his hotel over the summer and was friendly with the manager's niece. She worked in the office and she told me Mr Carter had specified his own suite of rooms himself because he used them to work in when he was staying at the hotel. He took a personal interest in the whole building. Everything was run by him first."

"You see?" said Vilho. "Taking a more detailed approach now could bring dividends in the future. My thought is that we design one or two apartments far more thoroughly than we would normally do at this stage."

Christina nodded, following his logic perfectly. "Your cutaway drawings, perhaps. Do you have time?"

"I can make time. We can work until late tonight. Will Nanny will give us dinner?"

"Certainly. She'd love to."

Paul stirred. "Yes," he said in a measured voice. "A case where it is important to get the initial design accepted. Good luck, I will be interested to see the results. I'm afraid we are out this evening or I'd offer to help." He nodded genially and left.

"Giving us his blessing," muttered Christina sourly.

Lucy cleared her throat. "My fiancé is collecting me here when I finish work. I'll let you know when he arrives, shall I? It will be quickest if we share a cab to Edgar Mansions."

"That sounds very efficient. Thank you." Vilho nodded to her in a friendly fashion and she withdrew.

Jack took the change of plan in his stride as Lucy had been confident he would. It wasn't until the two architects were measuring her slip of a kitchenette and talking in quick sentences between themselves that he drew his beloved out of earshot and asked what the idea was.

"I didn't say anything at the time," began Jack.

"I knew you wouldn't. You have such nice manners."

"I'm told a great deal of effort went into my upbringing. To return to this evening, as a piece of research it's a stroke of genius inviting your employers here, but you looked as though you'd seen a ghost when I arrived so there has to be more to it than that."

Lucy's mouth was dry as she remembered. "I did see a ghost in a way," she said. "Miss Kent's door was open when I went up with the tea and I heard her and Mr Kent arguing. He was there on Saturday, Jack. At the Black Cat club. Miss Kent said he was wearing his new overcoat and I suddenly remembered Miss Hodge saying he always wore a different one when he was at White City. I asked her later and she says it was a red and grey check."

"Like the one Milcombe *wasn't* wearing, you mean?"

"I know it's jumping to conclusions again, but what if the coat itself was a visual code signal to the drug peddlers? That's not really the point though. I think it had to be him I saw arriving at the Black Cat club, but even if it wasn't, Miss Kent *told* him she saw him leaving. She'd parked her car in a side alley, she said, and he walked right past it."

"Visiting Rose?"

"He denied the whole thing and said he was at home. But Jack, a sister knows her own brother. If it had been me, I wouldn't have been able to mistake Aidan whatever he was wearing. And then I remembered him saying on the phone that he couldn't do something on Saturday because he was dining out with his wife. I also remembered Mrs Kent at the gallery saying they hadn't gone somewhere at the weekend because he hadn't been well and they had an early night, but she blushed as she said it, so maybe it wasn't illness, maybe he'd persuaded her to give the dinner party a miss and then slipped out late that night."

By the intent, calculating look on Jack's face, he was coming to all the same conclusions Lucy had been dazzled by earlier. "I wonder... I learned today that Daisy saw what she thought was Milcombe's coat hanging in the side passage. Enid said it was gone later. Kent would know all about that passage. Uncle Bob will need to check on the pattern. He'll also need to establish exactly where Kent was between ten pm and midnight."

"Phone him, Jack. Think how dozy I was last night. If I'd been asked to swear in the witness box that you'd never left the flat, I wouldn't have been able to. If Mr Kent gave his wife a sleeping pill in her evening coffee, she'd never know he was out."

"True."

"Anyway, right or wrong, I dashed into the draughtsmen's office to gabble an invitation to Mr Koivisto. He practically dragged me into Miss Kent's room to say what a good idea it was." She held Jack's gaze. "Don't you see? The important thing is that Miss Kent is going to be busy all evening and not alone tonight. I couldn't have lived with myself if I hadn't made sure of that."

Jack lifted her hands and kissed them. "You are my very best girl and I adore you."

"There's something else. Mr Kent had a Black Cat matchbook on Monday, but Enid said they'd only been delivered on Saturday."

"It may have been an old one. Keep our guests busy while I get Uncle Bob on the telephone and then we can all go and view the downstairs flat that Vickers has already decided we should take."

"You've only just caught me. I was about to go home. We've made an arrest in the City robbery, so as I didn't sleep last night..."

"Can you bear to put it off?" Jack quickly filled his uncle in on the potential new development.

"Typical. We interview everybody leaving the club at midnight, and a witness turns up that we didn't even know was there. Write me a report and bring it over tomorrow."

"Can't you at least talk to Kent's valet or the St John's Wood servants? Find out if he went out on Saturday night?"

"Not just on your word. It's circumstantial. I do remember the name Koivisto in the visitor's book, but he left earlier. I'd better have him and Miss Kent in when I've got a free moment."

"Earlier than that if you can manage it. It hangs together, Uncle Bob. Forrest wants to sell out his interest in the Black Cat club. Rose is desperate to keep it in her own hands, so was nagging Milcombe to come up with the money. Milcombe won't spend a penny of his profits on anything except his horses, so was pressuring Kent to repay the loan he made him."

"Go on," said his uncle, scepticism rolling down the line.

"When Kent says he doesn't have the money, Milcombe says all right, you can help me make some instead. Come and collect more of my packets of drugs and deliver them to my contacts at White City. He lied about going there too, don't forget."

"I'm not forgetting. There is no evidence he collected more drugs."

Jack despaired. Lucy was quite sure Kent was dangerous. In the hallway, he heard her say she'd just find him, then they could view the new flat. "Wait," he said slowly to his uncle as she slipped into the room. "There might be evidence of a sort. Did you look at those letters I brought over from the Consolidated Cocoa office?"

"Not yet."

"Do so. If I'm right, the race-track pushers were always told to send their payments to PO Box 47, giving their code name so Milcombe could tick them off. Those would be the names marked 'WC' on the list."

"Agreed."

"But the latest letters to PO Box 47 said the money had been given to the bearer."

Across the room, Lucy's eyes widened as she put two and two together. Her hand went to her mouth.

"Meaning?" His uncle's voice cracked out like a whip.

Jack took a deep breath. "Milcombe would never have stood for that. He didn't trust his couriers one iota. You know it and I know it, and all we've done is to watch him at a distance. Paul Kent had known him since school.

He *knew* Milcombe would put the heavies on him if he pocketed the payments. Uncle Bob, whoever told those pushers on Monday evening to give the money straight to him, knew Milcombe was dead."

There was a longer pause. "It still won't hold water. Rose could have written to Kent before Monday. She could have telephoned and told him. She was desperate for money to get the club into her own hands, as evidenced by her contacting you so quickly over selling that horse."

"Didn't you have a tap on the club phone?"

"We did," said Curtis grimly. "It was quietly cancelled and the trail obscured, meaning someone in my own organisation is being persuaded to avert the cause of justice. That's my problem, not yours, but it's another reason to believe the place is a significant conduit for drugs. We'll borrow Arama for that if not for anything else."

"What are you going to do about Kent? Lucy says he had a book of matches on him that weren't delivered to the Black Cat until Saturday."

"Damn you, Jack. All right, I'll work on it."

CHAPTER NINETEEN

Long before dawn, Christina wrapped her dressing gown around her and went downstairs to where Vilho was still working at the large table in her room.

He looked up and smiled, making her heart turn over. "You are supposed to be sleeping."

"I have slept for two hours, which is more than you have. I'll make us some tea. How is it going?"

He nodded towards the litter of papers on the table. "I'm enjoying it. Take a look."

She picked up the topmost cutaway diagram. Lucy Brown's kitchenette sprang into life before her eyes, but not in any way the designers of Edgar Mansions had ever envisaged. A wave of admiration and joy swept through her at the talent embodied in this man. "Vilho, it's perfect. I'll get the tea. Then we should talk."

When she came back, he had shuffled all the papers together and was reading through them. "It is enough for Carter, I think."

"He cannot fail to be impressed. Vilho, are you too tired to discuss something? I have been thinking that if Paul does not express remorse for stealing our designs or show any signs of acknowledging the severity of what he has done, I will find it very hard to continue working with him."

Vilho sipped his tea. "I too. It will be painful to sever the connection after such a long association, but we both know what your brother is like. He will smile and laugh and promise and not alter his ways at all. The only way to force a change would be for you to threaten to dissolve your partnership, leaving us to set up on our own. Paul knows he would not last six months without us."

Christina smiled ruefully. "He could manage without me, he would merely need to employ a bookkeeper. He could not manage without you. Yours are the inventive designs that carry us forward."

"As always, you are too modest. You are the heart of this practice. See how he is after the meeting this morning. Nothing will be signed today, so if Paul is still obdurate, we can walk away and come to an arrangement with Mr Carter ourselves. If he is as much of a businessman as Lucy reports, he will not commit to any firm that has just lost their best designers."

"I hope so," she said anxiously.

"Does it worry you, the thought of starting out anew?"

Christina shook her head. "No, not with you. We have the expertise. It is simply such a very large step."

The door opened. Nanny stood there, also in her dressing gown with her grey hair pulled into a plait over her shoulder. "Thought as much," she said. "I've put eggs, sausages and bacon on for both of you. There's time to bathe and dress before it's ready, Miss Christina."

It was the same voice that had brooked no nonsense for the past forty years. Christina stood obediently and was both gratified and surprised when Vilho rose, stretched and hugged the elderly woman.

"The gods themselves could not ask for more. Will you cook for us and nag us when we are married, Nanny?"

Colour rose in Nanny's thin cheeks. "I'd like to see how

you'd manage if I didn't. Get away with you, Mr Vilho, and mind you bring that crockery upstairs for me to wash."

Lucy got ready for the day in a fraught rush of trying not to forget anything. "Will our life be less chaotic when Vickers is organising everything?" she asked.

"Worse," said Jack. "He'll sit us down and make us eat breakfast, then present you with a list of new garments you should be buying during your lunch hour."

Lucy glanced at him apprehensively, unsure whether he was joking. "Are you sure we can afford the bigger flat?"

"You might have to double your typing speed."

"That bad? Ah well, I've only got another week, then I can write full time. For the moment, anyway. Oh, look at the time. I must fly."

"Off you go then. Take care. I've got a busy morning ahead myself."

At work, Miss Hodge was full of weekend plans. "Frank is taking me to the cinema tonight and said he'd like to come dancing tomorrow. I'm being careful, though. I'm sure he's all right, but Dad said I should always see the colour of a chap's money before I let him take me dancing, even if he is his own apprentice."

Lucy chuckled. "Sensible advice. The only thing my father did when I left home was to give me a horseshoe to keep in my handbag."

The younger woman beamed. "That's lovely. Was it to bring you luck?"

"No," said Lucy. "It was to wallop anyone who tried to take liberties."

Miss Hodge shrieked with laughter, then stifled it and became very busy taking her typewriter cover off as Miss Kent came in.

"Good morning, ladies. Miss Reed, could you let me

know as soon as Mr Kent arrives? I need to discuss the revised plans with him before the meeting." She smiled around the room, looking tired, but poised and full of purpose. "I don't think I'm giving too much away to say it's an important day today. I wonder if you would mind very much bringing in the refreshments yourself, Miss Reed. Mr Carter could be an extremely influential client. Nothing against the rest of you, but I feel he would appreciate the attention of our most valued and senior member of staff."

Miss Reed flushed, very pleased. "Certainly, Miss Kent. I'm sure we all hope the meeting will go well."

"Thank you. If it doesn't, it won't be for lack of preparation. Mr Koivisto was up all night working on the plans."

She nodded to them and withdrew. Lucy sat down behind her typewriter, breathing a silent sigh of relief. Given the circles Jack moved in, it was not impossible that she would one day meet Mr Carter socially. She would far rather he didn't recognise her from all the various jobs she had done in the past.

Paul breezed into the room looking every inch the cheerful, successful architect. It was, thought Christina drily, an illusion he perpetuated very well.

"Good morning. Here I am. Run the plans by me, Vilho, and then I suggest you cut off home and get some sleep. You look exhausted."

"I will manage, Paul."

Paul gave a genial chuckle. "How long have we been friends? I know you won't have slept all night. Off with you as soon as we finish. We can let you know this afternoon how the meeting went. Where do we start? What do I need to present Carter with first? This one? Oh, very nice.

Beautiful work. Quite exceptional." He reached for a pad of paper and began to make quick, succinct notes as Vilho explained the various concepts.

Christina's lips tightened. There was no one better at grasping the essentials of a project straight away and then presenting it to clients, but she could already see her brother was going to take the whole credit for the idea when they met with Mr Carter and his associates. Behind his back she mouthed "Copper Grill" at Vilho. He nodded slightly, then gestured for her to take the chair next to him, them on one side of the table, Paul on the other.

Jack let himself into the Consolidated Cocoa office. He hadn't had time the previous afternoon to do more than write Mrs Antrobus a receipt for the key, lock up, then rush across town to meet Lucy after work. Keeping his gloves on, he carefully folded a note that was on the desk and put it in his inside pocket, transferred quite a number of items to his own office next door, and locked up again. He had enough to do this morning without spending most of it checking through paperwork. First came a visit to the twenty-four hour tailoring outfit next to the Black Cat club.

"Yes, sir," said the elderly assistant who came shuffling out from the back room to the counter, "certainly we can copy a coat for you if you leave it with us for a day or so."

"Yes, but how will I know if you can do it accurately," said Jack, affecting a fretful manner. "Is there someone you've done something similar for who can give a testimonial, so to speak?"

The tailor jerked his thumb sideways. "Gent from the club next door. Said he wanted a couple of overcoats made. You could go in and ask him. Bluff sort of man. Very good humoured. Paid in cash." The tailor sighed nostalgically.

"Thank you, I'll do that," said Jack. He tipped the man and left. He did not, however, go into the Black Cat club. He walked past the chophouse, took a ruminative look at the alley, then hopped on a bus heading east.

The meeting had gone well. Christina shook hands with Mr Carter, murmured that it had been a pleasure working on such an exciting project, then stepped back as her brother saw them off exuberantly from the front door.

"Paul, I need to talk to you about..."

He strode past her into his room. "Can it wait until this afternoon? I'm running frightfully late. It was worth the extra effort though, don't you think? Pretty sure we've got that one in the bag."

"It's really quite important..."

"Later, Christina. Nothing is ever that important. Good job Carter doesn't need entertaining to swing the deal. Business hours only. I'd have had to put my other client off. Off for your walk, eh? See you this afternoon, then. We can plan out the schedule."

He wasn't going to admit to the theft of their work. He would never admit it. He would pretend nothing had happened at all. Mechanically, Christina put on her coat, adjusted her hat and smoothed her gloves. She thanked Miss Reed for her discreet way with the refreshments this morning, pulled the door closed behind her and paused on the steps. She felt an absurd instinct to turn on her heel and run upstairs to her safe, familiar workroom. The world suddenly seemed too large, too bewildering, full of uncertainty. Was this how agoraphobics felt going outside?

Get hold of yourself. Remember when you left Radlett, with Nanny and all your worldly possessions packed into the car, and moved in here. You were confident then. You were

your own woman, knowing you were doing the right thing.
You still are.

Christina's head went up and she walked briskly towards the Euston Road. It was as busy as always there, so much traffic, so many people, everybody intent on their own lives. An open sports car with a long, low bonnet roared past, causing the horse pulling a butcher's cart to shy.

"Dangerous beasts," grumbled a woman to her right. "Shouldn't be allowed."

Christina moved slowly along, hampered by the lunchtime crowd. Women shopping, talking about a pot of tea and a bun. City gents, important in their uniform of hats, gloves and umbrellas. A boot black, plying his trade next to a water trough.

She stopped, looking across the road. In the Copper Grill opposite, Vilho's profile was clearly visible through the glass. She caught her breath. It was now or never. As the traffic surged, halted, surged again, she saw the space between them almost as an isthmus connecting everything she had always known on this side, everything she had ever thought to be true, with an unknown country on the far pavement.

The traffic eddied, paused, a slender gap opened up. Christina stepped off the kerb. And felt herself fall as something hooked itself with deadly accuracy around her ankle.

During the next few confusing seconds, she was aware of certain things very clearly. First a lean, strong arm smelling of boot polish catching her and hauling her upright just before a bus thundered past. Second, a sound like a handbag with a horseshoe in it connecting with the side of someone's head. Third, a pleasant voice saying, "I don't think so, sir. Not this time. Let's get these cuffs on you and we can have a little talk at the station." And finally Vilho, paler and more romantic than she had ever seen him, exploding across the road to crush her against his chest.

It was a full hour since Paul Kent had been arrested and taken to Scotland Yard for questioning. Lucy, ferrying yet another tray of tea into Miss Kent's room, was struck by how pale and stricken both she and Mr Koivisto still were. The fierce elderly housekeeper from upstairs who had evidently been Miss Kent's nanny at one time, bustled in after her with a plate of cake.

She nodded approvingly at Lucy. "Pour it out, dear. Now, I want you both to take a slice of this plum cake. Do you the power of good after a shock like that."

"He tried to kill me, Nanny." Miss Kent glanced helplessly at Jack, sitting very much at his ease on one of the bench seats and looking disturbingly attractive in his boot-black outfit. "Even after all we discussed last night, when you explained your reasoning and we arranged the details of the... of the trap, I didn't think he really would."

"Nasty child," commented Nanny briskly. "You can't bring a boy up from the nursery and not know. Charming as you like as long as he got his own way, and would go to any lengths to make sure he *did* get it. Think of that poor chap who died while Miss Marion was still deciding who to accept. Your mother knew. It's my belief that's why she made you promise to look after him and your father."

"What if... what if they let Paul go?" Miss Kent's voice shook.

"There are men downstairs right now changing the locks on all the doors," said Lucy quickly.

"They won't let him go," said Jack at the same time. "Half a dozen unimpeachable witnesses saw him follow you along the pavement and quite deliberately reverse his umbrella to hook your ankle, causing you to fall into the road."

"Eat the cake, Miss Christina. Drink your tea. You too, Mr Vilho."

Miss Kent picked up her cup obediently, then met Lucy's eyes. "The wages envelopes are in the end cupboard," she said. "I made them up last night while Vilho was working, just in case... in case..." She took a steadying breath. "Will you distribute them, please, and tell everyone they may have the rest of today and tomorrow off. I find there is a limit to how possible it is to carry on as normal. Come back when you've done it."

Lucy nodded and pressed the invisible catch to release the cupboard door. She was instantly swept back to the week before. *This was how it had all started.* "This was how it started," she said aloud. "Your cupboards in the Black Cat club and Jack finding the packet of drugs in the bench seat Mr Kent had been sitting on."

"I want to hear it all," said Miss Kent. "I won't sleep unless I know."

"A lot is informed guesswork," began Jack as Lucy slipped out of the room with the wage packets. "It started, we think, with Mr Kent needing money..."

By the time she came back, Jack was saying, "So there you are, Milcombe was desperate for money to stop Rose plaguing him when Forrest decided to sell out. Kent knew Milcombe would go to Mrs Kent and bring his house of cards crashing down if he didn't find him the cash. Milcombe more or less ordered him to collect more dope on Saturday night for distribution so he pretended to have a headache to get out of the dinner party. When his wife decided to stay home with him, he slipped her a sleeping tablet and went out once she was asleep. Chief Inspector Curtis has spoken to the valet. The servants were told to go to bed, but he and the footman stayed up playing cards and heard the side door. Apparently they were used to their master slipping out at night and thought nothing more of it. The valet confirmed the chequered overcoat had been worn."

"That coat, so unlike him."

"We think Milcombe had copies made for his couriers to wear. Pushers were told a man wearing such a garment would be at a certain place. The money was then sent to the Belgravia post office for Milcombe-Trelawny to collect, but that's by the by. The point is that Kent saw the opportunity to get rid of Milcombe and be free of his debt."

"And free from being at someone else's beck and call," put in Vilho musingly. "It makes sense, Christina. Paul hates not being in control. Can the police prove it?"

Jack hesitated. "Not as it stands. He will certainly be convicted of Miss Kent's attempted murder, but as for the attack on Milcombe... Uncle Bob is going to question the eye-witnesses again. It is my belief that as soon as she sees which way the wind is blowing, Rose will turn King's Evidence, admit she was out of the club at the time and saw Kent push her husband."

"Is it in her interest to do so?" asked Lucy.

"Oh yes, did I forget to tell you? Uncle Bob raided the club and arrested Youssif Arama who is falling over himself to say the drugs were all Milcombe's idea. Rose is claiming complete innocence. The only thing she wants is enough money to buy the club and to run it herself in her own way. The sooner the murder is pinned to Kent and she is no longer a suspect, she can do that by selling Milcombe's racehorses."

"Paul will deny it."

"Yes," said Vilho gently, "but you *saw* him there, Christina. You placed him in the right place, at the right time. You are a key witness, and thus a danger to him. Your brother is ruthlessly self-centred. We have always known it. I, myself, was sure the moment he told me this morning to go home and get some sleep. Only my absolute faith in Sinclair, Lucy and the police persuaded me away from your side."

Tears began to roll down Miss Kent's face. Vilho held her to him, rocking her softly. He looked up. "I will look after her now. Everything will be most unpleasant this weekend, but we will come through it stronger. Thank you, Lucy. Thank you, Sinclair. Thank you both for all your help. We will see you on Monday."

The building was quiet as they left. Everyone had taken their unexpected holiday and gone.

"I don't know about you," said Lucy, "but I'm exhausted."

"No time for that. We've got work to do." Jack hailed a cab.

"What sort of work? Jack, this isn't the way to Edgar Mansions."

"Correct. You and I are going to make hay while Uncle Bob is busy."

She eyed his boot-black's outfit. "Dressed like that?"

He looked down at himself and sighed. "So practical. That's what I love about you. Back to the flat first, so I can change into something more suitable."

CHAPTER TWENTY

"My last week," said Lucy to Miss Hodge on Monday. "Have you heard from your friend? Is she better? How did your weekend go?"

While Miss Hodge chattered away about how Smithy was much better, thank you, and that she'd had a grand time and Frank-the-apprentice was a right laugh and a good dancer, Miss Reed came in. Lucy saw at once that the older woman had suffered a great shock but was holding herself together in the manner of disillusioned ladies everywhere.

"Miss Kent will address the staff this afternoon," she said. "It's not my place to say more, but things are going to be a little different from now on." She moved to her table and sat down, then looked across at Lucy. "Incidentally, Miss Brown, I don't know whether your fiancé made enquiries about those investments, but I received a very disappointing letter on Saturday. Consolidated Cocoa has stopped trading. A cheque had been returned to me for my full stake money."

"Oh, that is a shame," said Lucy sympathetically. "An investment-broker friend of Mr Sinclair's advised him to put his money in gilts. Slow, but steady, is how he described the returns."

Miss Reed sighed. "I daresay he is right."

In obedience to Miss Kent's request that she serve mid-morning refreshments to herself and Mr Koivisto early, Lucy took their tray up before starting on the rest of the workforce.

Miss Kent smiled wanly when she came in. "Thank you. It has been a very trying weekend. I believe we have drunk an entire shipping container of tea between us."

"It must have been so horrible for you."

"Awful. As if we had never known Paul properly at all. My father feels it keenly."

"The higher the pedestal, the greater the shock when it crashes down," murmured Mr Koivisto.

"He aged, I think, twenty years in as many minutes. What was striking was that he never once questioned Paul's guilt. He blames himself for indulging him from an early age, for not diverting my brother's ruthless streak into more civilised channels. The legal repercussions will reverberate for quite some time. Meanwhile, we are to be married very quietly at Radlett as soon as it can be arranged. Vilho will become a partner and the practice will be known as Koivisto and Kent, Architects. We are hoping that our reputation for innovation and excellence will get us through the scandal of having a former partner tried for murder."

"I am sure the company will go from strength to strength," said Lucy.

"We have high hopes. You will be pleased to hear your suggested approach to Mr Carter on Friday has borne quite spectacular fruit. We are to sign the contracts and start work as soon as may be. He has also hinted that if he expands his Kingsthorpe interests, he may consider Vilho's modular homes. I believe he fancies to rival the Lever enterprise at Port Sunlight."

"Oh, how marvellous. I was sure when he heard your

enthusiasm in person he would choose you over anyone else."

"What puzzles me, Lucy - I may call you Lucy, may I?"

Lucy nodded. "Please do."

"What puzzles me is why you are so interested in our work? You are clearly not simply a typist."

Lucy felt herself blush. "I didn't set out to mislead you. I'm a novelist. I write career books and detective stories. I wanted to know what being an architect was like, whether it was possible for a female to become one. I wanted to know the sort of things architects do, what goes on inside a practice. Getting a temporary job inside my chosen setting is how I usually manage my research."

"Inefficient," said Vilho, picking up a biscuit.

Christina Kent threw him an affectionate grin. "Indeed. It sounds very time consuming. Why did you not make an appointment with me and ask?"

Lucy stared at them, feeling extraordinarily foolish. "That never occurred to me."

"As things turned out, I cannot say I am sorry. I suppose you would not like to research life as a housekeeper, would you? Mrs Drake is leaving to live with her daughter and I have to interview for a new one. It will not be an easy task. My father hates change and will find fault with all the applicants in an effort to persuade Vilho and me to move back there to look after him."

"Which we will not," said Vilho firmly. "We will find Garth a new housekeeper if we have to interview every woman in England."

"They will have to be thick-skinned. His latest grumble was to accuse Mrs Drake of pilfering his medication."

Lucy was visited by an idea. "Would you consider asking Mrs Corrigan? I told you her landlord has put up their rent and she is worried sick about how they will manage. She said she use to work here before the war.

Would Mr Kent remember her? I think she would prefer to be a housekeeper than a typist and she was telling me her husband would fare much better if he could get out in the air and do some gardening. The children are very well behaved."

Miss Kent's face lit up. "That is an excellent thought. I will ask her. Papa will certainly remember her and there is a cottage in the grounds they could have, though it will need some work doing to it. It would, however, leave us one typist short..." She looked at Lucy consideringly.

Laughing, Lucy shook her head and prepared to return downstairs. "I'll stay this week until Miss Smith is back, but after that I've got books to write."

It was late Wednesday evening when Chief Inspector Curtis made an unheralded visit to Edgar Mansions.

"Evening, Lucy. Finished at that architects' practice yet?"

"Not until Saturday. Why?"

"Things might be more cockeyed than usual tomorrow."

At his tone, she instinctively reached for Jack's hand.

"Don't tell me you're granting Kent bail?" said Jack.

"Hardly. He was found dead in his cell this evening. He'd taken a massive overdose of a very strong sleeping drug."

Jack stared. "In police custody? That was a slip up on your part."

"Nothing of the sort," said Curtis, sounding nettled. "There was nothing on him when we picked him up. He was very thoroughly searched."

"The tablets could have been sewn into his suit," suggested Lucy. "Miss Kent said her father had been complaining some of his medication was missing. Mr Kent could have taken it."

His sideways glance told her his opinion of the far-fetched ruses detective story writers dreamt up.

"Dead, though," said Jack. "That's a hell of an admission of guilt. Had he had visitors?"

"Only his solicitor."

Lucy thought about Mr Kent, his charmed life, his massive self-belief. "I suppose he couldn't face the thought of the court. It's better this way, but I can't help feeling for his wife."

"His wife was the one who arranged the solicitor," replied Curtis.

Lucy blinked. "Good heavens."

"She tells me she has been devastated by the whole affair, her nerves are in pieces, she may never recover and she and her daughters are returning to America where she hopes they can put the horror and the disgrace behind them. She is a wealthy woman in her own right, of course."

"It sounds as though they were equally ruthless," said Jack. "If she sent the overdose via the solicitor, Kent would have known she had no intention of standing by him. I imagine he decided falling asleep and not waking up was an easier option than the big drop. Shame you won't get any more from him about Milcombe's drug operation."

Curtis stretched. "I doubt he knew any more. We've rolled up as many contacts as we got our hands on. Young Aidan Brown's information was useful. Apart from maintaining it was all Milcombe's idea, Arama is keeping his mouth tightly buttoned. Rose is likewise maintaining her innocence on the drugs front and we can't do a thing about it. She's entitled to everything Milcombe left."

"She'll sell the horses and buy out Forrest," prophesied Jack. "The Black Cat club was all she wanted. Did she see Kent push Milcombe?"

"Undoubtedly, but she's covering herself by admitting she did walk a short distance with her husband, parted

215

from him in good spirits and when she looked back, saw him talking to a chap in a red and grey checked coat who *could* have been Kent but was too far away for her to identify."

"If she tried that line on Mr Kent, she was lucky she didn't have an accident too," said Lucy.

Curtis nodded. "I feel it would only have been a matter of time. By the by, Jack, did you ever give me back the Consolidated Cocoa keys? I ought to tidy that office up along with the rest of the Milcombe case."

Jack looked vague and stood up to check his jacket pocket. "Sorry, here they are. I forgot them in the confusion. I meant to give them back to you on Friday."

Lucy, remembering their frantic filling in of cheques and the typing of envelopes until late on Friday, preserved a tactful silence.

"I read your piece in *The Times* about the various ways these low-stakes confidence tricksters hoodwink their investors. Strong, but made a lot of good points. Nicely handled, nephew."

Jack shrugged ruefully. "For the best effect it should be reported in the same rags that are running the adverts. Unfortunately my contract with *The Times* means I'm obliged to offer them first refusal on any articles."

"All that lovely extra income going begging," lamented Lucy. "Ooh, Phoebe could report that she caught up with the famous 'Curtis of the Yard' recently, and he told her the police are cracking down on plausible criminals who are preying on hard-working people. It's not 'Society Snippets' fare but I bet they'd like it."

Jack's eyes gleamed. "They would if you phrase it in the best *Courier* style. Phoebe could send in a regular 'Crime Chat'. Four inches a week on handy tips to stay this side of the law and hang on to your cash. How about it, Uncle Bob?"

"Sometimes, the pair of you appal me. Regrettably, the idea has merit. I'll think about it."

After Curtis had left, Lucy said, "What about our office? The Elljay one?"

"I thought we might keep that going. Useful to have somewhere neutral for undercover shenanigans. I can work there when you're sick of the sight of me at home."

Lucy smiled. "It's a deal. I'm definitely not taking on any more temporary jobs until I finish this book. Maybe the next one too."

"Certainly the next one too," replied Jack. "We'll need your advance for the rent."

"What I love about you is your romantic soul."

"I solemnly promise to unchain you from the typewriter for the whole duration of our wedding day. Talking of which, the Lester double wedding is next month. They live relatively close to my folks. Mother wonders whether you would like to stay with us and go as part of the family group?"

Lucy came back down to earth with a bump. "Won't it be horribly grand and best-behaviour?"

"Count on it. Mrs Lester is set on outdoing Veronique Carter's wedding to the Earl of Elvedon. Church ceremony first, then grand reception and ball at Theo Nicholson's eccentric cousin's place. Stay overnight, limp home next day."

It could be useful to see a society wedding and grand ball at close quarters.

We-e-e-ll..." she said.

"Excellent for copy," he added seductively, walking his fingers up her arm.

Lucy ignored the ripples of interest his fingertips were creating and pretended to consider. "In what way?"

"Eccentric cousin Winnie lives in a fortified, moated manor. Gothic enough to give you nightmares. I stayed there as a boy, once. Theo's terrified she's going to die one day and bequeath it to him. Do say you'll come with me."

A gothic manor? She nearly whimpered at the research possibilities. "Would you like me to?"

He slid an arm around her. "Very much. Apart from anything else, you can set a murder book there. *Terror in the Turrets.* I can see it now."

She grinned. "You are such a charmer. All right, I can do grand for one day."

"Pack a notebook. Mrs Lester will have organised everything for maximum effect. Unlike our wedding, which I would prefer to be small, intimate and largely for us."

Lucy relaxed into his embrace. "Even if we lose the ring, the best man gets into a fight and we have to have the wedding breakfast in the nearest café because the church hall has slid into the Thames overnight?"

"Indisputably. That would be a wedding to remember. The twins' one will be forgotten in six months. I'll look for a suitably perilous church hall tomorrow."

She felt herself shake with laughter. It was as she'd known all along. Marriage to Jack was going to be anything but ordinary.

~ ~ ~The End ~ ~ ~

ACKNOWLEDGEMENTS

As I finally reach the end of this book, I have various people to thank. Firstly, the National Archives at Kew for a wealth of knowledge about nightclubs during the 1920s

Second, Lev Parikian for unwittingly supplying the very words I needed to unlock the concluding scenes of the story [via his utterly joyous "World Cup of Random English Words" on Twitter which brightened a very gloomy 2022]

An enormous thank you to Louise Allen for her support, encouragement and eagle eyes

Thanks also to Sheila McClure for ongoing cheerleading and general madcapness, not least of which was the parcel of cake which arrived at precisely the right time

Especial thanks to Kate Johnson, not only for her never-ending support and friendship, but also for providing the exact phrase to describe the costumes worn by the Kitten Kaboodle. Genius with words, that woman

Thank you to Jane Dixon-Smith another splendid cover

and thank *you*, if I've forgotten to include you

WORKS BY JAN JONES

Full Length Novels

STAGE BY STAGE – Cambridge set romcom featuring
a musical theatre company

A QUESTION OF THYME - herbs, healing and
humour: love story with WW1 incursions

DIFFERENT RULES - living, loving and growing in a
1990s Bohemian vicarage

~ Smoke and Mirrors ~

MYSTERY ON THE PRINCESS LINE - 1920s
ocean liner mystery

MYSTERY AT THE BAY SANDS HOTEL - 1920s
coastal resort mystery

MYSTERY AT THE BLACK CAT CLUB - 1920s
London nightclub mystery

~ Newmarket Regencies ~

THE KYDD INHERITANCE
– secrets and skulduggery in Regency England

FAIR DECEPTION
– secrets and scandal in Regency Newmarket

FORTUNATE WAGER
– secrets and sabotage on the Regency racecourse

AN UNCONVENTIONAL ACT
– secrets and subterfuge in the Regency theatre

~ Furze House Irregulars ~

A RATIONAL PROPOSAL
- cads and card-sharps in Regency England

A RESPECTABLE HOUSE
- scars and scoundrels in Regency Newmarket

A SCHOLARLY APPLICATION
- mysteries and missing persons in Regency Newmarket

A PRACTICAL ARRANGEMENT
- horrors, hopes and happy endings in Regency England

Novellas

THE PENNY PLAIN MYSTERIES

quirky, cosy novellas, set in a harbour town on the edge of the English Lake District

1: THE JIGSAW PUZZLE – old jigsaws, switched paintings, new friendships

2: JUST DESSERTS – ice-cream, jam wars, a lost aeroplane and the WI show

3: LOCAL SECRETS – graffiti, town planning, a local brewery and a WW1 mystery

4: THE CHRISTMAS GIFT – pilfering, old photos and a memorable Nativity

Other novellas

WRITTEN ON THE WIND
– trees, old ways & mobiles set on the N.Yorks moors

FAIRLIGHTS – a pele tower overlooking the sea, secrets stretching back for years

WHAT THE EYE DOESN'T SEE
– a Flora Swift mystery set in a village post office

AN ORDINARY GIFT – a time-slippish paranormal romantic mystery, set in Ely

ONLY DANCING
– a romantic suspense, with 1970s flashbacks

Non Fiction

QL SuperBASIC – the Definitive Handbook

ABOUT THE AUTHOR

Award-winning author Jan Jones was born and brought up in North London, but now lives near Newmarket, equidistant from Cambridge, Bury St Edmunds and Ely. She writes contemporary, mystery, suspense, paranormal and historical romance.

Jan is a vice-president of the Romantic Novelists' Association, who are without doubt the loveliest band of professional writers anywhere on the planet. Their unfailing support and friendship is unrivalled, their parties are legendary and the annual conference is completely unmissable. Website at https://romanticnovelistsassociation.org/

Jan has won the Elizabeth Goudge Trophy twice (in 2002 and 2019), the RNA Joan Hessayon debut novel award in 2005, and has been shortlisted five times in various RoNA Romantic Novel of the Year categories. She writes books, novellas, serials, poetry and short stories for women's magazines. She can be found at http://janjones.blogspot.co.uk/ and is at https://www.facebook.com/jan.jones.7545 for Facebook and on twitter as @janjonesauthor

Fun fact: A former software engineer, Jan co-designed and wrote the Sinclair QL computer language SuperBASIC.

Her textbook '*QL SuperBASIC - the Definitive Handbook*' occasionally turns up in second-hand sales, commanding ridiculous sums of money and causing her to wish quite fervently that she'd kept her original author copies. Thirty years later she retyped, reformatted and re-released a Kindle edition of '*QL SuperBASIC - the Definitive Handbook*'. To her astonishment, and with heartfelt gratitude to all those in the QL community, it is still selling steadily.

Printed in Great Britain
by Amazon

23967738R00131